Katahdin:
Maine Murder Mysteries

William Graham

© October 2020 William Graham

All Rights Reserved

Other Works by William Graham

Poetry
Vox Publica
Terra Incognita
The Places You Can Go: Poems for Children
Amoricon and Other Poems
Smugglers' Notch
The Sweetest Swing: Baseball Poems
Interlude
Work: Labor Poems
Gathered Leaves: Selected Poems
A Good Place to Wake Up: Vermont Poems
The Love Poet of Vermont
The Storm Subsides: 50 Poems of Passion and Protest
Mountain Springs: Haiku from Vermont
Lengthening Shadows
Wolf Moon

Young Adult Fiction
Danny Boyle and the Underland
Danny Boyle and the Ghosts of Ireland
The Boy with the Golden Arm
Volcano Island
Kid Island
Olivia Turner's Amazing Amazon Adventure
Maddie the Dog

Fiction
Fire and Ice
Newfoundland Sagas
The Red Planet Trilogy: Three Novellas
The Red Planet President: A Novella
The Last Inning: A Baseball Novella
Greenfields: A Novella
Smoking Mountain: A Novella
Martian Darkness: Four Detective Ace Sloan Mysteries
Atacama Red: A Pablo Nelson Mystery
The Green Mountains Murders: A Detective Sophie Junot Novel
The Devil You Know: A Detective Sophie Junot Novel
Gilded Crimes; A Detective Sophie Junot Novel
Under Currents: A Detective Sophie Junot Novel
Bluff City
The Kincaids
Moose Island: Maine Murder Mysteries
Cadillac Mountain: Maine Murder Mysteries

Travel
Seven Continents: A Travel Memoir
Border Crossings: Travel Essays and Poems

Biography

Poet, novelist, and travel writer William Graham holds a BA and MA in English and a MS in Communication from Northwestern University in Evanston, Illinois. He lives in Stowe, Vermont.

PART 1: HELLFIRE AND DAMNATION

1

Ever since her divorce five years ago from Drew McCaslin, Lisa McCaslin always seemed to be short of money. In the divorce settlement, Lisa was awarded the one-hundred-and-fifty-year-old farm house just outside of Chesterville, Maine. But even with alimony and child support payments from Drew, she had a hard time paying the mortgage, utilities, and grocery bills for herself and her ten-year-old son Devin. Lisa worked as a substitute math teacher in the grade school in Millinocket, whose population of less than five thousand made it the bustling metropolis in this region of Maine's vast north woods. To supplement her income, Lisa also worked nights as a clerk at the Katahdin General Store, the manager of which was her high school friend Bonnie Coleman.

For the past year, Lisa had contemplated selling the house in the country and moving into an apartment in Millinocket, but Devin loved having the large yard that was surrounded by the vast forests. She couldn't bring herself to deprive her son of that lifestyle. But to maintain the bare necessities, Lisa had to spend a great deal of time away from her son at night while she worked at the store. Devin, however, was an independent and resilient child. When Lisa was working, he stayed home alone, except for the nightly visit by Lisa's nearest neighbor Carrie Holcomb, who had agreed to check in on Devin on the nights that Lisa was away. A widow for the past five years, Carrie loved getting out of her own empty house and spending time with Devin, who reminded her of her own two grandsons who now lived in Portland, Maine.

Carrie was a member of a devout congregation of evangelical Christians called The Flock, who worshipped at a small church in Chesterville. Carrie believed in the realities of hellfire and damnation. Even though she was happy to perform her Christian duty to help out her neighbor Lisa, Carrie cast an unapproving eye on the fact that Lisa appeared to have no religious faith and that Devin had not been baptized. During the few minutes each night during the week when she checked in on Devin, Carrie sometimes brought up the topics of Jesus Christ and sinners, but Devin politely, and skillfully for a boy his age, deflected the conversation to other more benign topics.

Devin sometimes mentioned these conversations to Lisa, who explained to Devin that Carrie was an old woman who had very strong religious beliefs.

"She means no harm," Lisa explained to Devin. "I just don't believe in the things that she does. If she makes you uncomfortable, I can tell her to stop coming over to check on you."

"No, that's all right," Devin said. "I look forward to her stopping by while you're at work. I feel safer knowing that she'll be coming by."

"That's the whole point. I have to work at nights to make money. I feel bad about leaving you here alone, but I have no choice. I wish I didn't have to. I'm hoping that a full-time teaching position will open up during the next school year," Lisa said.

"Am I going to stay with dad this weekend?" Devin asked.

"You know the routine," Lisa replied.

Drew McCaslin, an optometrist, owned a successful practice in Millinocket. The catalyst for the divorce five years ago was his affair with one of his assistants, whom he subsequently married. In spite of the fact that Lisa now considered him a cheating pig, he did take his paternal responsibilities seriously. He had promised to take Devin canoeing and camping in the Allagash Wilderness Waterway for the weekend.

With Devin gone for the weekend, Lisa could spend time with her new boyfriend Carl Seaver, who was an auto mechanic for the local Chevrolet dealership. Lisa had known Carl since they had attended high school together. They became reacquainted when Lisa brought in her SUV to be serviced. Carl was once a high school football star whom all of the girls had wanted to date. Though still handsome, Carl had packed on a few pounds now that he was in his early thirties. But then again, Lisa mused, she was no longer the skinny math whiz to whom everyone came for help with their geometry and algebra questions. Even though time had altered their once youthful, vigorous appearances, Lisa and Carl had a good time when they were together.

For now, however, Lisa kept her relationship with Carl a secret from Devin. She wasn't sure how serious she was about Carl at this point. So, she didn't want Devin to think that Carl could possibly become his stepfather. Lisa liked having Carl around on Friday and Saturday nights to share a pizza and watch horror movies, a genre that they both enjoyed.

After Drew had picked up Devin for the weekend trip to the Allagash, Carl came over, still smelling slightly like motor oil. He had brought a pizza and a six-pack of Sam Adams lager. He and Lisa settled in for the evening. Halfway through the movie, Lisa paused it and began kissing Carl, who responded in kind by pulling down Lisa jeans. Just as things were about to become interesting, Lisa saw a face staring at her through the window. She screamed, and then abruptly pushed Carl sway.

"Did I do something wrong?" Carl said.

"I saw a face at the window," Lisa said.

"Are you sure?"

"Yes. I'm not blind."

"I'll go check it out. Where's your flashlight?"

"In the kitchen drawer," said Lisa.

Less than two minutes later, Carl came back in the house, carrying a red gasoline can and a box of matches.

"Look what I found," Carl said.

"Jesus. Was someone trying to burn the house down?"

"It looks that way. Was the person you saw at the window a man or a woman?"

"I'm not sure. The face appeared for just a second," Lisa said. "Should we call the sheriff?"

"I didn't see anybody out there. What's the sheriff going to do?" Carl said. "Let's just make sure all of the doors are locked tonight."

"I usually never bother locking up at night way out here."

"Well, maybe you should start, especially on those nights when Devin is here alone," Carl suggested.

"Should I be worried, Carl?"

"I think it was probably a prank. Some bored high school kids. But if anything happens again, you should definitely contact the sheriff," Carl said, moving back on the sofa next to Lisa. "Now, where were we?"

"You have to be fucking kidding," Lisa said. "Let's watch the end of the movie and go to bed."

***

On an abandoned logging road, a half-mile from Lisa's house, a group of people gathered in the darkness around a small bonfire. They held thick leather-bound books in their hands. One person after another recited a passage from the book. "Sinners will be damned to eternal hellfire," one woman said. To which the others silently nodded their heads.

2

Shelley Gastineau preferred cutting men's hair rather than the locks of women. Men were less fussy, and she was able to see more clients in a day at Patty's Salon for Men, which was started four years ago by her best friend Patty Conroy. Of average height with a stocky build, Shelley proudly displayed her tattoos of red roses that ran up and down both of her muscular arms. Even though she had developed a steady clientele over the years, being a hair stylist was by no means lucrative. Her parents encouraged her to attend college after graduating from Millinocket's public high school, but she knew she was not cut out for undergraduate life. Plus, she admitted to herself, she was a homebody who didn't want to stray too far from her hometown and the vast north woods that surrounded it.

The Gastineau surname was well known in the area; her father Buck Gastineau was the sheriff of Penobscot County. Buck had always doted on his youngest child, who was the only one of his three children who had remained in the area. He was also very suspicious of the men Shelley dated since she was in high school. Without telling his daughter, Buck ran background checks on each and every male with whom Shelley had shown any romantic interest. If Buck found them unworthy, he met with them privately behind Shelley's back, telling them sternly to move on. Shelley never did discover why so many men abruptly dumped her without even a call.

The one man whom Buck found worthy for Shelley was Carl Seaver, who was hard working, honest, and an outdoorsman. Shelley felt the same way about Carl. On their first date in October nearly three years ago, Carl suggested to Shelley that they climb the nearly mile-high Mount Katahdin, which loomed on the horizon like a giant whale. The day had dawned clear and warm, but as the pair ascended the boulder-strewn slopes of what the indigenous people called the "Greatest Mountain," a cold front suddenly moved in from Canada. The wind began to howl like an injured animal and a furious rain began to pelt the couple as they neared the summit. Carl said they needed to get off the mountain as soon as possible. But on the descent, Shelley twisted her ankle. Carl could not get any reception on his cell phone. So, Shelley leaned on Carl for most of the next two hours as they made there way back to the trailhead, freezing, wet, and exhausted.

When Shelley told her dad Buck about this episode, he told her in no uncertain terms: "Marry this man." It took longer than just one terrifying incident on Katahdin for Shelley to fall completely in love with Carl, however. But a year into their relationship, Shelley was wondering when Carl would pop the question. But the question never came. Shelley began talking about having children, which only served to push Carl away. Eventually, Carl admitted to Shelley that he wasn't looking to get married or have children. He was content with his life the way it was.

The day after Carl ended his relationship with Shelley, he awakened to find his truck sitting in the driveway with its tires slashed and windows broken. The week following, he discovered the word 'Pig' spray painted on the side of his house. Acts of vandalism in various degrees of severity occurred over the next three years. Carl knew who had committed the acts of petty vengeance, but he said nothing.

He did nothing. He knew that Buck Gastineau would protect his daughter. Eventually, the harassment stopped. He figured that his strategy of just ignoring Shelley completely had worked. She clearly wanted him to react, to explode so that her father could arrest him. He wasn't going to take the bait. He went on with his life. He had found a new barber. And now he had found a new girlfriend in Lisa McCaslin.

***

Lisa was a heavy sleeper. She referred to it as the 'sleep of the dead.' Carl, however, was an anxious sleeper; he was one minor sound away from jumping up and being ready for action of some sort. A week after Lisa had allegedly seen a face staring at her through a window, Devin was once again away for the weekend with his father. Carl shot up in bed after hearing a sound coming from the backyard of Lisa's property. Without waking her, he descended the stairs and went outside. In was early September. Low clouds dropped from the sky, blotting out any moonlight or starlight. He heard the snap of dry twigs coming from the woods at the end of the lawn. It could be a raccoon or a deer, Carl thought. He heard the sounds again. They came from behind the tool shed next to the small garden. Carl walked on the cool grass in his bare feet. He slowly opened the door of the shed. Then he was struck on the head from behind. He crumpled to the floor of the shed, banging his head against a shovel and a rake that stood next to the entrance.

"What the fuck," Carl muttered.

He then smelled the distinct aroma of gasoline, followed by an explosion. And then heat. The shed had been set ablaze. He staggered to his feet before the shed became engulfed in flames with him inside of it. He ran back toward the house searching for a garden hose. He yelled for Lisa to wake up. But he received no response.

He eventually connected the hose and doused the flames. But the shed was two-thirds charred.

He returned to the house and finally awakened Lisa. He explained to her what happened.

"This time I'm contacting the fire department and the sheriff," Lisa said. Then she observed: "My god, there's blood all over your T-shirt."

***

"How's your head, Carl?" Buck Gastineau said. "By the way, nice to see you again."

"The EMTs said I'll be fine. No stitches needed. It looks worse than it is."

"But somebody clocked you really good," Buck said. "You didn't see who did this?"

"Nope."

"Do you or Lisa have any idea why someone would set her shed on fire?"

"We have no idea," Carl said. "But a week ago, I found a gasoline can and matches in the yard. We must have spooked the person then. But he came back again."

"Jim Hines the fire marshal has been looking into several suspicious fires around town in the last few months. This could be related. We think it's a group of teenage boys who don't have anything better to do," Buck said.

"Do arsonists usually assault people?" Carl said.

"No. You have a point there," Buck said.

"Lisa is really freaked out," Carl said.

"I'm sure she is," Buck said. "In the morning I'll have one of my deputies look through the woods for any evidence and canvas the area."

"I'd appreciate that."

"So, Lisa is a fine-looking woman," Buck said. "Are things getting serious?"

"I don't know. What does it matter to you, Buck?"

"Now, don't take my inquiry in the wrong way, Carl. I'm just making friendly conversation. Shall I tell Shelley you said hello."

"Do whatever you want, Buck."

3

Austin Miller looked over at his coworker Lou Holmes as they lifted boxes containing various auto parts into a truck that then delivered the parts to car dealerships and auto repair shops in northern Maine. In his early thirties, Lou already was showing signs of a crooked back and the onset of early arthritis in his joints. He told Austin that he pounds down pain killers with a glass of whiskey every night when he returns to his single-wide mobile home.

At nineteen years old, Austin wondered if he was looking at his future. After graduating from high school, Austin found a job as a pizza maker and delivery boy at

Roma's Pizza. But as he told a friend: "The wages were shit. And people in this town don't tip worth a damn." Through a friend, he heard that North Woods Auto Parts was looking for a warehouse employee. The only qualifications were a strong back and legs and the ability to not get on the bad side of the manager Ron Collins.

After a year hoisting boxes into delivery trucks, Austin had managed to keep his job and even receive a dollar an hour raise. But whatever he earned was not enough. He had to support himself and supplement the meager government payments received by his invalid mother Audrey, who spent her days lying in bed, usually with a cold wash cloth on her forehead to ease the pain of debilitating migraine headaches. Austin's father, who once earned a decent living as a logger, had deserted the family without a trace ten years ago, about the time Audrey joined the religious congregation called The Flock. Austin's father thought that the worshippers were certified nut jobs. But Audrey believed that the congregation had special powers that would relieve her pain. Ten years later, however, Audrey was still waiting for God's grace to cure her. So, until a miracle occurred, she counted on welfare payments, Medicaid, and food stamps.

After completing work, Austin drove home in his used Chevy truck that was already showing signs of rust. One of Ron Collins's friends had helped secure him a significant discount on the vehicle. Even though Labor Day had just passed, the leaves were already beginning to change color and a noticeable chill was in the air. Home for Austin and his mother was a small, two-story, white clapboard-sided house that had needed painting for the past ten years. After Austin's father had left, Austin helped his mother move her bed from the master bedroom on the second floor to the living room on the first floor. This is where Audrey spent her days with the blinds closed and watching cable TV with the sound turned down to a barely audible level.

"I brought home some fried chicken and potato salad from the grocery store," Austin said.

"Please put a few pieces of dark meat on a plate for me," Audrey said. "And bring me a Dr. Pepper. Can you also give me my hair brush? Carrie is coming over later so we can read Bible verses together. I want to look presentable."

On the nights when Carrie visited for Bible study with his mother, Austin decamped to his room to watch YouTube videos or Red Sox games on his phone until Carrie departed and his mother had fallen asleep. When Austin was certain that his mother was asleep, he departed the house to make his nocturnal rounds of burglary. Tonight, he headed for the vacation cabins in nearby Twin Lakes. The solitary structures that were scattered in the woods were ripe for the picking, and they would be empty. After breaking in, Austin searched for electronic devices or sports equipment that could easily be sold online.

Austin was so focused on the task at hand while inside one cabin that he didn't even hear the crunch of gravel outside. As he exited the cabin carrying a flat-screen TV, he was blinded by a light from a flashlight.

"What the fuck!" Austin yelled.

"Good evening, Austin," Buck Gastineau said. "Enjoying your evening out? Just look at those stars. Makes you want to weep they are so beautiful."

"Shit," Austin then muttered. He had encountered Sheriff Gastineau several times in the past after having committed petty drug offenses that resulted in no more than a small fine. But now Austin realized that he could be in deep shit.

"How did you know I'd be out here?" Austin said.

"I've been getting reports from home owners of property thefts. I decided to stake out this area tonight," Buck said. "I guess I hit the jackpot. You sell that stuff online?"

"Maybe."

"Where do you store it?"

"In my tool shed at home."

"Your mother know about what you're doing?" Buck said.

"What do you think?"

"She would think you're a sinner, Austin. Doing the devil's work."

"That's about right," Austin said. "So, are we going to stand here and chat? This TV is getting heavy. Or are you going to arrest me?"

"I'm going to make you an offer. I'll forget about these break-ins. You cut me in on fifty-percent of what you get," Buck said.

"Why would you do that?"

"These home owners can afford to replace this stuff. Most of these cabins are owned by doctors or lawyers from Bangor, Portland, and even as far away as Boston. But you know as well as I do that making a decent living around here is tough. A person has to scramble, to improvise to make ends meet. That includes your humble county sheriff. What do you say, Austin?"

"If it's a choice between going to jail or cutting you in, my answer is pretty obvious," Austin said.

"A sound judgment on your part," Buck said. "I'll set up a time and place weekly for us to meet. Cash transactions only. I don't want an electronic trail. Have a good evening now."

***

Austin's tasks for the evening weren't finished, however, after his business deal had been struck with Sheriff Gastineau. He had received a text message earlier with an address he was supposed to go to. He knew the place. It was an establishment called Good Stuff that sold adult sex toys. He pulled a gasoline can out of the back of his truck and got to work. Twenty-minutes later, he had showered and then burrowed under the covers on his bed. He looked at his phone. In four hours, he had to be at the warehouse to fight his way through another monotonous day. The last thing he heard before he had fallen asleep was the sound of sirens cutting through the night.

4

Drew McCaslin's second wife Roxie left Drew's optometry practice after the birth of her first child Brendan. Two years later she gave birth to Seamus. Within the first few months of becoming a mother, she noticed that Drew was not being as attentive to his infant son as he was to his older son Devin. Drew brushed off the criticism. But in Roxie's mind the pattern had continued when Seamus arrived. Roxie felt that all of the parenting responsibilities were falling on her shoulders. And she didn't want to spend her days in the grinding cycle of changing diapers, making dinners, and cleaning the house. As the spouse of an educated professional man, she wanted to keep up appearances, specifically her own.

She convinced Drew to hire a local woman to help her with the house cleaning and the child care, allowing her the freedom to take cycling classes and to attend hot yoga sessions. That is, when she wasn't getting her nails manicured and hair styled. She wanted to maintain her lithe figure and to keep Drew's eyes on her alone. Truth be told, she still felt jealous of Lisa, even though Drew had divorced her five years ago. She felt that Lisa was using Devin to keep a hold on Drew. During the times when Lisa dropped Devin off for the weekends, she felt that Drew and Lisa were a bit too chatty for her taste. There was still a lingering emotion in their glances, Roxie believed.

Over time, Roxie's resentment of Lisa festered. On one of the nights that she had to prepare dinner for the family, she realized that she didn't have all of the ingredients necessary for the lasagna recipe that Drew particularly liked. Roxie dashed to the Katahdin General Store, forgetting that Lisa worked there most nights. She immediately spied Lisa standing behind the cash register. She avoided eye contact as she searched for the ingredients she needed in the far aisle.

After filling her basket, she knew that she now had to interact with Lisa. It's hard to hide in a small town. The past catches up with you eventually.

"Hi Roxie," Lisa said. "Is that all you are buying today?"

"Yes. I just made a quick run here. I'm fixing Drew's favorite dinner," Roxie said.

"Since you're here, just a reminder that I'll be bringing Devin over on Saturday morning," Lisa said as she scanned Roxie's purchases. Lisa couldn't help but notice Roxie's perfect nails and her slim waist. She wondered if Drew maintained a separate bank account just to underwrite Roxie's vanity.

"I meant to text you, but since I'm here I'll just tell you," Roxie said. "Devin can't stay with us this weekend. I have plans to visit my parents in Bangor. My mom broke her ankle a few days ago. Handling three boys would be too much for Drew. Plus, I want him to spend more time with just Brendan and Seamus."

"But Devin was expecting to go fishing again with his father."

"Well, things have changed. Not everything revolves around Devin. It's best that he figures that out now," Roxie snapped.

"Here's your stuff," Lisa said, pushing the plastic grocery bag at Roxie.

"The service here is so pleasant," Roxie said.

Now Lisa really had no choice but to introduce Devin to Carl Seaver. She felt nervous about the prospect. But, she thought, she liked Carl so it might be time to gauge how Carl and Devin got along.

***

The combination of being disappointed about not spending the weekend with his father and the nervousness about meeting Carl caused Devin to be unusually quiet, which made for an awkward dinner with Lisa and Carl. Devin picked at the pizza that Carl had brought.

"I thought you liked the pizza from Roma's," Lisa commented.

"I'm just not that hungry I guess," Devin said, eyes downward. "Can I go to my room now?"

"Sure, honey," Lisa said.

"Do you think he likes me?" Carl asked Lisa after Devin had left the table.

"Most kids are shy when they meet someone for the first time. Plus, he's mad that his stepmom Roxie wouldn't let him stay with Drew. Apparently, Roxie thinks that Drew is too brittle to watch over three boys for twenty-four hours," Lisa explained.

"That Roxie is a piece of work. I see her strutting around town like she's a runway model," Carl said.

"I'll never know what Drew sees in her," Lisa said.

Carl was savvy enough not to respond. He knew exactly what Drew saw in Roxie.

***

Usually a light sleeper, on this night Carl was dead to the world through a combination of too many beers and an extraordinarily warm quilt that Lisa had pulled out now that nighttime temperatures had consistently fallen into the low thirties. By the time Carl awoke, the house was fully engulfed in flames. He poked Lisa to awaken her. The bedroom was filled with smoke. Carl felt the intense heat as he and Lisa made their way down the hallway to retrieve Devin, who was still asleep.

Carl jerked Devin from his bed.

"We have to get out of here!" Carl yelled at Devin. "The house is on fire!"

Katahdin

The trio descended the smoke-filled stairs. As they reached the bottom, a portion of the ceiling collapsed, striking them with heavy, burning beams. Lisa screamed. She couldn't find Carl or Devin amidst the burning debris. In spite of the flames licking her clothes and bare skin, Lisa pulled piles of wood off of Carl and Devin. Coughing and bleeding, Carl was able to stand up and carry Devin. He and Lisa ran through the front door and into the front yard. Carl placed Devin on the cold grass. Devin was not moving or breathing. Lisa attempted to resuscitate him, but there was no response.

Carl had enough wits about him to have grabbed his phone from the nightstand. He called 911 as Lisa frantically tried to revive her son. Carl noticed that his skin was singed and bruised. But he and Lisa were alive. He could hear sirens approaching. That sound, however, was drowned out by Lisa's piercing cries.

***

"There's been an incident in Millinocket," Captain Davies informed Nadine. "A young boy was killed in a house fire."

"What does that have to do with us?"

"The fire marshal confirmed that the fire was deliberately set. So, it's now a murder investigation. I'd like you to take the case," Davies said. "I'll let the local sheriff Buck Gastineau know that you'll be arriving tomorrow."

"It's a small town. Somebody must know something," Nadine said.

"Small towns can often hide big secrets," Davies said.

5

Nadine met Sheriff Buck Gastineau at the still smoldering remains of Lisa McCaslin's home. A cold autumn drizzle began to fall as Buck showed Nadine around the property.

"The fire investigator said the blaze began on the back porch, fueled by several gallons of gasoline," Buck said. "The fire spread very quickly through the wooden house from there."

"I'll be talking to Lisa McCaslin this afternoon. But has she told you who she thinks could have done this?" Nadine said.

"She has no idea," Buck said.

"I'll also need to talk to her boyfriend Carl Seaver. He's already been released from the hospital, correct?"

"That's right," Buck said.

"I hope that I will have your full cooperation in this investigation. A young boy died needlessly," Nadine said.

"I'm at your service, Detective McAfee."

"Before I arrived here, I learned that there have been several mysterious fires over the past few weeks. Do you think this fire could be connected?"

"Possibly. But those other fires were at businesses. One was at a sex shop, and the other was at a women's clinic," Buck said.

"No clues were found at either location?"

"None."

"This fire seems personal since it involved a private home. The question is: Who was the target?" Nadine said.

"I couldn't say. Lisa and Carl are just normal people," Buck said.

"There is no such thing as 'normal,'" Nadine said.

Before heading to the Millinocket Regional Hospital where Lisa was recovering from burns and smoke inhalation, Nadine checked in at the Moosehead Lodge, which would be her home for the duration of the investigation. She requested a room with a view of Katahdin, a mountain she had climbed several times while an undergraduate at the University of Maine. She wasn't sure that her knees would be up to the task now, however. But seeing the grand mountain again brought back fond memories. She thought to herself that maybe she would try to climb Katahdin again.

After getting settled into her wood-paneled room that was adorned with multiple photos of moose, Nadine drove to the hospital. When she walked into Lisa's room, a man, whom she surmised was the boyfriend Carl, sat in the chair next to the hospital bed.

"Good afternoon, Lisa. I'm Detective McAfee from the Major Crimes Unit. And you must be Carl Seaver?" Nadine said.

"That's right," Carl said.

"I've been assigned to this case to find out who burned down your house. Let me say straight away that I'm sorry for the loss of your son. But I will find the person or persons who did this," Nadine said. "The fire was clearly set intentionally, and it led to the Devin's death. My job is to find his killer. And I need your help."

"I can't imagine who could have done this," Lisa said, wincing in pain.

"Can't this wait?" Carl said. "Lisa is still recovering."

Nadine noticed that a bandage covered the back of Carl's head. And he had nasty looking red burn blotches on his hands and forearms.

"I understand. I just have a few questions now. I know that there are pressing arrangements to be made," Nadine said. "Has anyone threatened you via phone or text messages?"

"No. No one," Lisa said. "But this wasn't the first fire on my property. A tool shed was set on fire and Carl was clubbed on the head. And before that, I thought I saw a face peering through a window. I couldn't make out who it was. But looking back on it, maybe that was a warning. But I have no idea who I might have offended. I really don't."

"And Sheriff Gastineau hasn't found any suspects?"

"No."

"What about you, Carl? Maybe the person who set the fire was targeting you," Nadine said.

"I can't imagine who," Carl said. "I'm just a humble auto mechanic."

"What about Shelley?" Lisa interjected.

"Now, Lisa. Don't start with that. This is way beyond what Shelley would do," Carl said.

"Who is Shelley?" Nadine inquired.

"Shelley Gastineau. My ex-girlfriend. We didn't have an amicable split," Carl said.

"Shelley's been harassing Carl for years," Lisa chimed in.

"What's Shelley's relation to Sheriff Gastineau?" Nadine said.

"She's his daughter," Carl said.

"Shit," Nadine muttered.

"But she has left me alone for over a year now," Carl said.

"Did you report the alleged harassment?" Nadine said.

Carl laughed: "Maybe you didn't hear me the first time. Shelley is Buck's daughter. He would have made my life a living hell if I had filed a formal complaint against Shelley."

"I'll still have to look into her possible involvement. Something may have set her off," Nadine said. "It's the only thing I have to go on so far. I'll be in touch."

On her way to talk to Shelley Gastineau, Nadine drove by the funeral home where the wake for Devin McCaslin would take place tomorrow. She could not fathom the grief that Lisa must be feeling. Nadine was certain, however, that the pain inside Lisa was more intense and would endure longer than her physical injuries.

"I'm looking for Shelley Gastineau," Nadine announced as she entered the hair salon. A woman with heavily tattooed arms emerged from a small room in the back of the establishment, which currently had no customers.

"I'm Shelley. I'm sorry, but we just style men's hair here," Shelley said.

"I'm Detective McAfee. I'm investigating the fire that killed Devin McCaslin. I'd like to talk to you."

"To me? Whatever for? I don't know anything about the fire, other than it was a terrible thing," Shelley said.

"You used to date Carl Seaver, correct?"

"That's right. A long time ago," Shelley said.

"Carl says that you used to harass him after the two of you broke up."

"I don't know what he's talking about. We may have exchanged a few nasty words, but what couple hasn't said things they regret when the relationship starts to go bad. Besides, he never reported anything to the police. So, it's my word against his."

"Did you know that Carl was dating Lisa McCaslin?" Nadine said.

"I guess."

"Maybe you realized that Carl had finally moved on. And that made you so angry that you decided to teach Lisa and Carl a lesson. But your plan got out of hand and a little boy ended up dead," Nadine said.

"I didn't start that fire. I wouldn't have," Shelley insisted.

"Where were you two nights ago?"

"At my friend Patty's house. She owns the place. She can verify that."

"Where's Patty now?"

"Out getting some food," Shelley said.

"What time did you leave her place?"

"Around midnight I guess."

"That still would have given you time to drive to the McCaslin house in Chesterville, set it ablaze, and then return to your apartment," Nadine said.

"I didn't burn that fucking house down!" Shelley screamed as Patty Conroy, the salon's owner, walked in carrying bags of Chinese food.

"What's going on here?" Patty said.

"I'm Detective McAfee. Was Shelley at your house two might ago?"

"Yes. Until around midnight."

"Shelley, I'm going to request that a forensics team go through your car and apartment. If you don't agree to the search, I can get a warrant," Nadine said.

"My father is the county sheriff. You must know that," Shelley said.

"That's old news to me. And irrelevant," Nadine said. "Will I have your cooperation or not?"

"Fine," Shelley said. "You won't find shit because I didn't start that fire."

***

Nadine couldn't bring herself to attend Devin McCaslin's funeral. She wanted to let the family have a private moment to grieve. Instead, she stayed in her room at the Moosehead Lodge going over the forensic team's report. Nadine was hoping to find evidence of gasoline or other accelerants in Shelley Gastineau's car or on her clothes. The team only found a stash of marijuana in Shelley's car. Nothing was discovered that could implicate her as the arsonist.

Nadine had begun a background check on Lisa's ex-husband Drew and his wife Roxie when there was a knock on her door. When Nadine opened the door, Sheriff Gastineau burst in.

"What the fuck do you think you're doing accusing my daughter of arson!" Buck yelled.

"I was following up on a lead. That's what I do," Nadine said, standing her ground. "Shelley had been harassing Carl Seaver for years. But, as Carl explained it, he never reported the incidents because he knew you would protect your daughter. Are you protecting her again now?"

"Fuck you," Buck said. "Shelley wouldn't burn a goddamn house down."

"But she would slash tires and break windows. That you can tolerate," Nadine shot back.

"You got any evidence tying her to the crime?"

"No."

"Then stay the fuck away from my daughter. And be careful who you accuse in this town," Buck said.

"Someone set that fire in which Devin McCaslin ended up dead. Who do you think did it then?"

"You're the star detective. I'm just a humble county sheriff. You tell me," Buck said.

"In time, I will," Nadine said. "Just don't interfere in my investigation."

"I wouldn't think of it," Buck said. He then turned around, slamming the door as he departed.

6

After Lisa had buried her son Devin, she moved into Carl's house. It would be months before she received the monetary compensation from the insurance company for the loss of her house. Living with Carl was her only option, although she felt that the move was still premature given the still casual nature of their relationship. Carl, however, proved a steadfast and congenial companion, especially given Lisa's violent mood swings in the immediate days following Devin's death.

Even though her injuries were not completely healed, she decided to return to work at the general store. She declined an invitation to substitute teach in the fall semester to replace a math teacher who had gone on maternity leave. Being around young children would spark emotions that would be too raw, she decided.

She continued with her night shift at the general store. During the day, she made Carl's house more livable, at least according to her standards. She gave his place a thorough scrubbing and dusting, made sure that all of the laundry was done, and even cut the grass in the yard.

"You didn't have to do all of this," Carl said.

"I don't know how long I'll be here. I like order," Lisa said.

"Was I that much of a pig?"

"I've seen worse," Lisa said, smiling.

Carl wasn't the only man with whom she had to contend, however. Even since Devin's death and burial, Drew had become especially needy. Lisa chalked it up to grief. Funny, she mused, how women were often portrayed as the more emotional. But it was Drew who couldn't seem to accept that his oldest son was now dead. Twice in the last week, Drew had insisted on meeting Lisa for lunch to reminisce about their marriage and their late son.

"This is all my fault," Drew said. "I should have let Devin stay with me that weekend."

"That's nonsense," Lisa replied. "You can't torture yourself. No one could have predicted what happened."

"I'm the one who destroyed our marriage. This is my punishment," Drew continued.

"We can't change the past. You are now married to Roxie and have two young boys to think about. And I've moved on, too," Lisa said.

"Do you have any idea who could have done such a thing?" Drew said.

"No. Do you?"

"No. Do you think that Carl was the actual target? We both know that he hangs out with a bunch of poker buddies," Drew reminded her. "Maybe he's in debt and couldn't pay up."

"Yes, I know that Carl likes his poker night with the guys. But he tells me that the stakes aren't that large. I can't imagine that a debt of a few hundred dollars caused someone to burn down my house. And we don't even know if he is in debt," Lisa said.

"I told Detective McAfee about Carl's gambling," Drew confessed.

"Why did you do that?"

"I think the detective should check it out."

"Carl will be pissed at me," Lisa said.

"If the detective finds nothing, that'll be a good thing," Drew said. "You can smooth things out with Carl."

"You better hope so," Lisa said, clearly annoyed. "Before we go, I'd appreciate it if you would stop calling me. We're divorced. Our son is dead. You have your own family. Having these meetings is weird and uncomfortable. What would Roxie think?"

"She doesn't know," Drew said.

"I wouldn't be so sure about that," Lisa said. "I have to go now. My advice is to start moving on. Devin is never coming back."

On the drive back to Carl's house, Lisa was so annoyed with Drew that she didn't notice that she was being followed. The vehicle stopped a block from Carl's house. The driver noted the house's street address and then drove away.

***

"We meet again, Detective McAfee," Carl said, wiping oil from his hands with a rag.

"I wanted to give you and Lisa some time to take a breath after Devin's funeral," Nadine said. "How's your head?"

"Just a few stitches and some clumps of hair that were singed. But the hair will grow back."

"Is there somewhere we can sit?"

"There's a picnic table out back," Carl said.

Carl guided Nadine through the noisy auto shop to a small plot of grass behind the car dealership where employees could eat lunch when the weather was good.

"What can I do for you?" Carl said.

"Carl, I heard that you like to gamble. Poker is your game of choice I believe," Nadine said.

"How do you know this?"

"It came up as part of my investigation."

"Did Lisa mention this to you?"

"It doesn't matter who told me," Nadine said. "How's your luck been lately?"

"It could be better."

"How much do you owe?"

"A few thousand."

"Could you be more specific?"

"Three thousand to be exact."

"To one person in particular?" Nadine said.

"Yeah. His name is Miles Offerman. He owns a construction company."

"Why can't you pay him back?"

"Let's just say I'm not the best guy when it comes to handling my finances. I had to put in a new furnace at the house before the winter arrived," Carl said. "And fix a drainage problem that was causing flooding in the basement."

"Is Offerman a patient man?"

"Fuck no. He's been on my back for weeks to pay up."

"Has he threatened you?"

"He said he would kick my ass. But that's just talk. Me and the other poker buddies don't believe him. When he's had a few too many, he can fly off the handle. But he knows I'll pay up eventually."

"Could he have assaulted you at Lisa's house? Could he have set the house on fire?" Nadine said. "Maybe it was one of those nights when he had a few too many."

"I just can't believe Miles would do that. And what would be the point? I couldn't pay him back if I was dead," Carl said.

"Sometimes it's not about the money. It's simply about revenge," Nadine said.

"Talk to him if you want. But I don't believe Miles could have done it," Carl said.

"People are capable of many things, Carl," Nadine said. "It's the dark side of human nature that keeps me employed."

7

Rusted-out cars and trucks, piles of lumber, metal scaffolding, and assorted pieces of construction equipment lay scattered amidst now withered weeds at Miles Offerman's construction company headquarters. But Nadine noticed that a brand-new Ford truck was parked outside. In the back of the truck were gasoline cans. Inside a concrete-block building sat Offerman, a man in his early sixties whose head seemed too large for his body. His fingers were stained with nicotine and he was missing two teeth. On Offerman's desk, amidst piles of rolled architectural drawings, sat a Bible that looked like it had been thumbed through heavily.

"What is your relationship with Carl Seaver?" Nadine said.

"We play poker. That's it," Offerman said.

"Is he a good player?"

"He doesn't play worth shit," Offerman said.

"He owes you money I understand."

"Yeah. About three thousand. I've been pestering him about it."

"Where were you on the night of the fire at Lisa McCaslin's home?"

"At Bible study with my wife. There were several dozen witnesses who could testify to that," Offerman said confidently.

"You're a religious man, Mr. Offerman? How does gambling fit into that?"

"I've been playing poker longer than I've been studying God's word. It was my wife who coaxed me into joining The Flock. It was either that or she'd leave me."

"What's The Flock?"

"It's a small congregation of Christians here in Chesterville. We come together for Bible study and Sunday services. We believe that only God can rid the world of evil. We are his servants in that effort to confront sinners wherever we find them. We ask them to repent," Offerman explained.

"But isn't gambling a sin?" Nadine said.

"I have this once vice. I've stopped smoking and drinking, for the most part. Well, sometimes the demon rum gets hold of me. But I like poker. It's my original sin, if you will. But I'm trying to stop."

"Do you think that Carl and Lisa are sinners?"

"Carl isn't a believer. He hasn't been saved. I know that. I can't account for Lisa."

"Did some other member of your congregation consider them sinners?"

"I couldn't say."

"I noticed that you have a new truck," Nadine said, abruptly changing topics. "You must be doing well."

"I know this place looks like a dump. But I'm doing all right."

"You have cans of gasoline in the back of your truck."

"I can see what you're getting at. I know you cops," Offerman said. "I didn't burn McCaslin's house down. In case you hadn't noticed, there's a whole lot of nothing around here. I sometimes have to travel long distances to job sites, or when I go hunting. I always keep a few spare cans of gas just in case there are no gas stations around. Most people around here do the same thing."

"Who is the minister of The Flock? I'd like to verify your whereabouts on the night of the fire."

"Her name is Ophelia Cannon. But everyone refers to her as Miss O," Offerman said. "I hope you find the sinner who started the fire. We prayed for the soul of the McCaslin boy."

"I'm sure your prayers made all the difference," Nadine said scornfully as she departed Offerman's office.

***

Ophelia Cannon had been ordained a minister after her graduation from a small Bible college in rural West Virginia, Nadine discovered after a cursory internet search. After leading several congregations in small towns throughout the south, she made her way to the north woods of Maine five years ago with an evangelical fervor to bring God to the vast wilderness.

With flowing gray hair, piercing hazel eyes, and an erect posture, Ophelia did not look like a religious zealot, Nadine thought. But then again, zealots came in all shapes and sizes. She lived in a small house that was attached to a similarly small, non-descript, and unadorned house of worship.

"God be with you, Detective McAfree. Call me Miss O. Everyone does."

"I think I'll stick with Reverend Cannon," Nadine said.

"I understand that there was a Bible study the night of the fire at Lisa McCaslin's home. Can you confirm that?"

"Yes. Everyone was there."

"Including Miles Offerman?"

"Yes. And his wife Debbie."

"What time did the session end?"

"Around ten o'clock at night," Cannon said.

"That would give Offerman or some other person time to torch the Lisa's house," Nadine said.

"Miles would never do such a thing. That would be against God's word."

"There have been other fires in the area in recent weeks. You wouldn't know anything about those blazes, would you?" Nadine said.

"Only that they have rid the world of sinful material," Cannon said.

"What was sinful about Devin McCaslin, the young boy who died?"

"You're assuming that the fires are connected," Cannon said.

"Maybe there are," Nadine said. "I'd like a list of all of your congregants."

"Of course. That will take me just a minute to print out that list."

***

In her room at the Moosehead Lodge, Nadine reviewed the activity of the sheriff's department over the past several months. In addition to the unsolved fires, there were a series of break-ins at vacation homes in the area for which there had been no arrests to date. While Nadine sympathized with the fact that Buck Gastineau had a small team of deputies, the number of open cases in the area raised an alarm in her mind. She called Captain Davies.

"What do you know about the county sheriff Buck Gastineau?" Nadine asked.

"Old Buck has a quite a reputation," Davies said.

"Of being what?"

"Of being lazy and turning a blind eye to some crimes to keep his case load down."

Nadine thought of Carl's comment that Gastineau had protected his daughter Shelley. Who else might Gastineau be protecting?

"Why are you asking?" Davies said.

"I'm wondering if Gastineau might know more about what's going on than he's willing to tell," Nadine said.

"I'd be careful about how to approach that subject with him. Buck has a temper."

"I've already encountered that."

***

Austin Miller's phone rang at the end of his shift at the auto parts warehouse. He listened carefully to the instructions he was given. Four hours later, after darkness had descended, he arrived at the back of Saint Thomas Catholic Church in Millinocket. He lifted a gas can from his aging Chevy truck that he hoped to replace soon. As he placed the can down on the ground, he turned and saw a figure emerging from the around the corner of church.

"Hey, what are you doing here?"

A gunshot hit Miller in the head. He fell to the ground next to the gas can. A full moon emerged from behind the clouds, bathing him in a soft yellow light.

8

Buck Gastineau was already standing over the body of Austin Miller when Nadine arrived at the catholic church.

"One of my deputies was patrolling the area, and he called it in," Buck explained. "I was here in five minutes."

"Who is the victim?" Nadine said.

"The kid's name is Austin Miller. Here's his wallet," Buck said. "Looks like we found the arsonist."

"Maybe," Nadine said skeptically. "But someone knew he would be here and executed him. Something doesn't add up. Did the deputy see anyone?"

"He says that he didn't," Buck said. "But I found a shell casing. I suspect the shooter probably used a Ruger. It's a popular handgun. Many folks around here carry one."

"I'll get forensics up here," Nadine said. "In the meantime, I'm going to go to the address on his driver's license. Do we know if he lived with his family?"

"Don't know a thing."

"Where's his phone?"

"I didn't find one on him," Buck said.

"Can you secure the scene and take care of the body?" Nadine said.

"Will do," Buck said.

Nadine drove to an address on Baxter Lane. She found it odd that Austin Miller, or anyone these days, would not have his cell phone with him. The device had become like another limb, always there. She arrived at a small house that needed painting. She pounded on the door. Eventually, Nadine saw that a light had been switched on. The door opened and a drowsy woman wearing old worn blue pajamas looked at Nadine.

"I'm Detective Nadine McAfee. Does Austin Miller live here?"

"Yes. He's my son. What's going on? What time is it?"

"Are you his mother?"

"Yes. I'm Audrey Miller."

"I'm sorry to inform you that your son was shot dead tonight. May I come in?"

Audrey motioned for Nadine to enter.

"Austin was shot? May God rest his soul," Audrey said. "Where? Who did this to my boy?"

"He was killed behind the catholic church in town. We don't know yet who shot him. He was carrying a gas can. We think he was going to burn the church down. We think he may have been behind the other fires in the area, including the one that killed Devin McCaslin."

"Austin would never do such a thing. He had no reason to."

"Did you know your son was not at home tonight?"

"No. I suffer from severe headaches, you see. I take medicine to help me sleep. I didn't hear anything."

"What about his father?"

"Hasn't lived here in years."

"Can you show me to his bedroom?"

"I need to lie down. It's upstairs on the right. Help yourself."

Nadine ascended a creaking set of stairs and entered a small unadorned bedroom that contained just a bed, desk, and clothes chest. Nadine looked around for a phone that might have fallen to the floor. Nothing. She then sifted through Austin's clothes. In one drawer, stuffed under some balled-up T-shirts, Nadine found a spiral notebook. In it was a list of various items such as computers, stereos, and televisions with prices noted next to them. Another column had a heading that read 'SG' with a series of dollar amounts beneath it. Nadine realized it was crude ledger of sales.

She returned downstairs, where Audrey was lying in bed with a wet face cloth on her forehead.

"Is there a garage out back?" Nadine said.

"No, but there is a small tool shed. You can go out through the kitchen door."

Nadine turned on her flashlight as she walked across the weed-filled backyard to the shed. She opened the door to find an inventory of electronic equipment sitting neatly on shelves. Nadine suspected that Miller had been burglarizing homes and selling the items online. She took photos of the goods and then returned to the house.

"Do you know what is in the shed?" Nadine said.

"I never go out there. Austin takes care of the yardwork," Audrey said.

"I found TVs, stereos, and computers that I believe Austin probably stole and then would sell online. See for yourself," Nadine said, handing Audrey her phone.

"I should have prayed more for him. My church should have prayed more," Audrey said.

"Do you belong to The Flock?"

"Yes. How did you know?"

"I've met a few of the members, as well as Reverend Cannon."

"When can I see my son?"

"I'll have Sheriff Gastineau contact you."

"God bless you. Find who did this to Austin."

***

"You have had quite a number of burglaries in the area, sheriff," Nadine said. "But I don't see any arrests. Why is that?"

"Remote locations. No fingerprints or witnesses," Buck said. "It's unlikely we would catch someone unless we just got lucky."

"Take a look at this," Nadine said.

"Where did you take this photo?"

"In a shed behind Austin Miller's house. And I found this notebook in Miller's room. It has a column for 'SG.' Who do you think the initials refer to?"

"I have no idea," Buck said calmly.

"I think 'SG' refers to you, Sheriff Gastineau," Nadine said. "Here's how I see it. You caught Miller one night.

Rather than arresting him, you cut a deal with him. Is that about right?"

"You have a fucking vivid imagination. You can't prove shit," Buck said.

"I'm going to get Miller's phone records. If I find something, I'll be turning over the evidence to the district attorney," Nadine said.

"Be my guest."

"Do you own a Ruger handgun?"

"As a matter of fact, I do. But you're way out of line if you think I killed that kid."

"I need to see the gun and have it tested by forensics."

"Again, be my guest," Buck said. "You're wasting your time on this. You're supposed to be here looking for an arsonist. And you found him: Austin Miller."

"I don't think he's the arsonist who torched Lisa's house, however. I think he was killed to deflect attention from the real culprit."

"Who is?" Buck said.

"I'm not prepared to say," Nadine said.

***

"I've received an angry call from Buck Gastineau," Captain Davies told Nadine. "Do you have any solid evidence that links him to Austin Miller? You can't just go around accusing a county sheriff of crimes."

"No," Nadine said. "Gastineau's gun had not been fired recently and there is no electronic evidence that Gastineau and Miller ever communicated. Gastineau knows how to cover his tracks."

"Then let it go," Davies said.

"I will. Even though I don't think he killed Miller, I do think he and Miller had an arrangement for splitting the proceeds from the burglaries."

"Even if you are right about that, there's no way to prove it now. Find the goddamn arsonist."

***

"Detective McAfee," Lisa said. "When Carl and I arrived home from a rare night out, we saw that someone had painted the words 'Burn, Sinners' on the side of the house in red spray paint. I'm afraid. And even Carl is shaken up about this. We're afraid that someone is going to burn Carl's house down."

"I'll be right over," Nadine said.

9

"Have you ever heard of a religious group called The Flock?" Nadine said.

"Yes. When I lived in the old house in Chesterville, one of my neighbors named Carrie Holcomb would come by the nights I worked at the general store to check on Devin," Lisa said.

"How did Devin like her?"

"Carrie is a nice woman. And I appreciated that she would take the time to look after Devin. But she would always try to convert me and my son. I laughed it off at the time," Lisa said.

"I've discovered that The Flock takes the Bible very seriously," Nadine said.

"You don't think they could be behind the fires and the murder of that man, do you?" Lisa said.

"As a matter of fact, I do," Nadine said. "Before coming to Maine, the minister, Ophelia Cannon, had some run-ins with police in the south. Something about harassing some of the locals who worshipped at other churches. The Flock has a cult-like pull on its members. I'm going to ask Sheriff Gastineau to post a deputy near Carl's house until I can gather further evidence."

"We'd appreciate that," Carl said. "In the meantime, I'm going to the hardware store now to buy paint to cover up those words. I'm not going to be intimidated by these people."

"Why do you think the word 'Sinners' was painted on the side of the house? Carl and I are law-abiding citizens. Neither one of us has been in trouble."

"Think about it. Carrie Holcomb or one of the other members of the congregation knew that the two of you were involved in a sexual relationship outside of marriage. That fact may have put a target on your backs," Nadine said.

"That's so puritanical," Lisa said.

"I'm just speculating. But I think that's why you were targeted. And Carrie had an insight into your lifestyle."

"But why target Devin also?" Lisa said.

"You told me that Devin usually spent the weekends at his father's house, correct? I think that whomever started the fire wasn't anticipating that Devin would be in your house on that Saturday night," Nadine said.

"How could someone live with the fact that they were responsible for a little boy's death?" Lisa wondered.

"People justify all sorts of things to themselves," Nadine said.

***

Nadine had trouble sleeping the night after Lisa and Carl had received the threat. Buck Gastineau had agreed to post one of his deputies in a car down the block from Carl's house. Finally deciding that sleep was futile, Nadine dressed and drove to Carl's house. A cold autumn rain assaulted the trees. Leaves had begun to litter the streets, sidewalks, and lawns.

Nadine parked a block behind the patrol car. She walked up to it. The car was empty. She noticed a light was on in Carl's house. She checked her phone. It was three o'clock in the morning. Keeping her profile beneath the height of the shrubs in Carl's front yard, Nadine peeked into the window. Carl and Lisa were tied up, surrounded by a group of four people, including the deputy that Buck Gastineau had assigned to watch over the house and Reverend Ophelia Cannon.

Creeping around to the back of the house, Nadine called Buck.

"What the fuck time is it?" Buck said.

"After three o'clock. I'm at Carl Seaver's house. Your deputy and three other people are in Carl's house. They have Carl and Lisa tied-up together. It looks like some kind of perverse trial is occurring. I could hear the minister reciting Bible verses."

"I had no idea that Deputy Streeter was a member of that church. He had specifically volunteered for the night shift," Buck said. "Shit. Now I understand why."

"Get over here now, sheriff," Nadine insisted.

"I'll be there in ten minutes."

"I hope Lisa and Carl have that long," Nadine said.

Nadine went around to the front of the house again to see what was going on. She spotted an older woman carrying a gasoline can. Could that be Carrie Holcomb? she wondered. The woman began spreading gasoline on the floor of the living room. The four members of The Flock then closed their Bibles and began walking toward the back of the house.

Nadine sprinted to the backyard to intercept the quartet as they exited.

"Police!" Nadine yelled. "Stop right there."

The deputy pulled out his service revolver and took a shot at Nadine. His bullet grazed the right shoulder of the rain jacket that she was wearing. But she was not injured. Assuming that the deputy was wearing a protective vest, Nadine returned two shots aimed at his lower body, hitting the deputy once in the right knee. He screamed in pain and crumpled to the rain-soaked grass. Nadine ran toward the fallen deputy and grabbed his gun. While the brief firefight was occurring, the minister had re-entered the house and started the fire. Nadine could see the flames and hear of panicked screams of Lisa and Carl.

"The sinners will now burn!" Ophelia yelled.

Nadine grabbed Ophelia by her hair, flinging her hard down the wooden steps that led into the kitchen. Two other members of The Flock stood mutely in the rain. A circle of flames raged around Carl and Lisa, each of whom had been secured by ropes to wooden chairs. Nadine began coughing as smoke entered her lungs. She felt that her hair was burning. She managed to make her way to Carl and Lisa and cut the ropes with her pocket knife. Nadine led the coughing couple out of the front door and into the rain, which had intensified.

"Are you both all right?" Nadine said.

"Yes," Lisa said. "But your face and hands are burnt."

"I'll be fine," Nadine said, as Buck Gastineau and another deputy arrived.

"In the back," Nadine said, coughing. "Deputy Streeter fired on me. I returned fire. He's been wounded. Three others from The Flock are standing back there, just waiting to be arrested, waiting to be sacrificed."

Buck ordered the other deputy to bring forward the group from the backyard.

"Let's get away from the house. The fire department and the EMTs are on their way," Buck said.

As the deputy escorted the four people, including the wounded Deputy Streeter, away from the house, now engulfed in flames, Nadine sat down on the wet curb as the cold rain pelted her.

"There are the people who burned down Lisa's house, sheriff," Nadine said. "And I suspect that you'll find that Deputy Streeter owns a Ruger that has been fired recently.

He killed Austin Miller to silence him and to throw us off the trail."

"The minister and the others look so calm, just standing there in the pouring rain," Buck said.

"Calm is not the word I would use. They look self-righteous. And now in their minds they'll be martyrs to their cause," Nadine said.

"You never know about people," Buck said.

"For once, I'll agree with you," Nadine said.

PART 2: LAND GRAB

10

Nadine was gardening when she saw a small fox slink out of the woods. The fox looked to be just a few weeks old. It staggered for a few feet after emerging from the trees, then plopped down in Nadine's backyard. The fox pup looked sick and hungry. Nadine suspected that the mother had abandoned it. Nadine knew that she should just leave the fox alone and let nature take its course. But she could not just stand and watch the fox die without trying to help. She went into the house and returned with a bowl of water, which she placed in front of the pup. The pup took a few sips and then closed its eyes. Nadine could see that it was still breathing, however.

Then the fox arose and slowly walked back into the woods. The following morning, Nadine noticed that the fox had returned once again to her lawn. Its breathing was shallow. She offered it water again, but the fox did not drink from the bowl. An hour later the fox pup had died. Nadine scooped up the dead fox with a shovel and carried it back into the woods, where she dug a grave. After placing the corpse into the ground, she covered it with heavy rocks so that no other creature could dig it up.

Even while relaxing at home, death seemed to find her, Nadine thought. The finality of death haunted her. She thought of her aging grandmother, who had to move to an assisted living facility after suffering a stroke. Nadine felt guilty about having moved out of her grandmother's house and purchasing a home in Porcupine Haven. If she had been with her grandmother, maybe she could have helped Martha. If she had been a better detective, maybe she could have brought justice to the victims of violent crimes. One of those crimes that bothered her the most was the so-called accidental death of Ruth Grove. Every day Nadine stared out at Mallard Island, where she believed that Sabine Grove killed her aunt and her aunt's personal assistant Amanda Wren. But she could never prove that Sabine was the killer.

Nadine wondered how much longer she could continue in her job with the state police. She began to lose sleep.

She decided to visit Martha, who was progressing in her physical therapy. She could now speak and she had regained movement on her right side. But she still lamented to Nadine that she had to sell her house, and that she was now confined to a small apartment in the assisted living building. But she was still alive, Nadine thought. Even though her tomorrows were limited, Martha still had something to look forward to, a luxury that the victims of the crimes that Nadine investigated didn't have.

***

You wouldn't know it to look at her, but Rhonda Quinlan had an estimated worth of nearly two-hundred-million dollars, a fortune that derived from her organic hand cream and soap called Nature's Balm, which she had recently sold to a French cosmetics conglomerate. She lived off the grid on a one-hundred-acre farm near Baxter State Park. On her property she raised chickens and goats. During the winter, her son Damien took care of the property while she traveled the world looking for warmer climes.

Two years ago, she purchased nearly ninety-thousand acres of land near Mount Katahdin, with the intention of donating the land to the federal government, which she hoped would establish a new national park. She had been aggressively lobbying President Osgood and his Secretary of the Interior. The purchase, however, irritated the logging companies and the local outdoorsmen, who objected to the land grab by this rich outsider from New York City no less.

Undeterred, Rhonda went about her business of maintaining her farm and writing letters to government officials. Short but muscular for a woman in her sixties, Rhonda wore tattered clothes and let her hair go gray. Her favorite uniform was her red plaid shirt that she wore almost every day in the cool summers of Maine's vast north woods.

On this day, she traveled into Millinocket to purchase additional wire fencing for the goats' enclosure. By now, most people in town knew who she was because of the local media coverage and her numerous appearances on national radio and television.

When she walked into the hardware store, she thought she heard someone mutter 'bitch' loud enough for her to hear. She looked around and saw a man standing in the aisle ten feet from where she stood.

"Excuse me, but if you have something to say to me, have the balls to say it to me face," Rhonda said.

"OK, if that's the way you want it. I called you a 'bitch,' because that's what you are. A 'rich bitch.' You think you can come in here and take all of that land," the man said. "My family and I used to hunt and snowmobile in that forest."

"The logging companies that were going bankrupt willingly sold the land to me. Maybe your beef should be with them," Rhonda retorted.

"It's all the same bullshit with you people," the man growled. "The land is for Mainers."

"Well, I think the land should be open for the enjoyment of all people, especially visitors, who will bring money into the area," Rhonda said. "But if you want to buy the land from me, make me an offer."

"Fuck off, lady," the man said.

When Rhonda took her purchase to the checkout counter, the store manager was not pleased to see her.

"Hey, I didn't start the trouble," Rhonda said. "And this is the only hardware store within fifty miles. Do you want my money or not?"

The manager wrung up Rhonda's purchase without saying a word.

When Rhonda arrived back at her property, she encountered two logs that were blocking the entrance to her private gravel road.

"Fuck," she grumbled. She made a quick call to her son Damien, who met her at the gate. Fortunately, Rhonda's truck had a winch on the front. She and Damien secured a winch cable to the logs and moved them out of the way as the truck backed up.

"When is this petty harassment going to end?" Damien wondered.

"Some people just want to live in the past," Rhonda said.

That night after completing her chores for the day, Rhonda sat in the living room of her farm house listening to National Public Radio. A shot rang out, shattering the large picture window. She leapt off of her chair and lay prone on the hardwood floor. Damien came downstairs from his bedroom.

"Holy shit," Damien said. "Are you OK, Mom?"

"Yes. Better call the sheriff," Rhonda said. "Somebody really doesn't like me."

11

"Damien," Rhonda said. "I just received a call from a producer at the *PBS NewsHour*. They want to send a reporter here to do an in-depth interview about my conservation efforts and my intent to donate the land near Katahdin to the National Park Service."

"That's great," Damien said.

"I think the interview should be conducted outside on the slopes of Katahdin and then in my acreage so viewers can see the beauty of the area."

"I think that's a great idea. When are the reporter and camera crew coming?"

"They'd like to be here next week," Rhonda said.

Prior to the scheduled interview, Rhonda conducted multiple conversations with the PBS reporter Samantha Guidry. Rhonda explained to Samantha that the area where she wanted to conduct the interview was rugged. Samantha informed Rhonda that she was bringing just one camera person who would operate a hand-held camera and a drone for aerial shots. Rhonda informed the *Millinocket Times* of the impending interview.

"Anything I can do to highlight the natural beauty of the region and to bring more tourists here to inject money into the local economy, I will do," Rhonda said.

Rhonda hosted Samantha and the camera person named Ron at her home the day they arrived. Ron recorded shots of Rhonda and Damien taking care of their animals on the farm. Samantha got some footage of Rhonda explaining her off-the-grid lifestyle.

"The weather tomorrow is supposed to turn cold and blustery in the afternoon, with a chance of a thunderstorm. A cold front is moving in from Canada," Rhonda explained. "So, we need to get an early start to get shots on the slopes of Katahdin and on my land just outside of Baxter State Park. I will warn you that the terrain can be rugged."

"We're prepared, I think," Samantha said.

The next day dawned clear and bright. Rhonda drove Samantha and Ron to a trailhead near Katahdin. The trio began the slog up the rocky path. Along the way, Rhonda stopped and answered questions about how reading Thoreau's book *The Maine Woods* had inspired her to move to the area and protect a large swath of land from commercial degradation.

After getting shots of the majestic mountain glimmering in the brilliant summer sunshine, Rhonda drove the group to a gate that marked the entrance to her ninety-thousand-acre refuge that she hoped would one day be part of the country's national park system.

"Acadia National Park on Mount Desert Island was once privately-owned land that was donated to the park system. So, there is precedent in Maine for doing this," Rhonda said. "I just want to do the same thing."

"What is the current status?" Samantha asked.

"I'm waiting for President Osgood to issue an executive order to permanently protect the land, which is in his power to do."

"What about the criticism that the land will be closed to hunting and other sports like snowmobiling; activities that are integral to the culture of the region?"

"I'm willing to work with local authorities and groups to possibly carve out some areas where different types of recreational activities are permitted on a limited basis. But I want the future park to be, for the most part, a place of quiet serenity where people can hike or canoe and just experience the silence of nature, where they can escape from the modern world," Rhonda said passionately.

After Rhonda finished her comments, Samantha called an end to the interview.

"This has been great," Samantha said. "Thanks for your time. The landscape here is stunning."

Just as those words came out of her mouth, a shot exploded the silence, striking Rhonda in the head. Blood, bone, and brain matter splattered on Samantha. The camera man Ron turned his camera to where he thought the shot had come. He managed to capture movement in the trees.

"Oh, my god!" Samantha screamed, as much for the sight of Rhonda lying on the ground with a large portion of her head gone as for the blood that had splattered on her clothes.

"I'm calling 911," Ron said. But he couldn't get a signal. "Fuck. I'm going to run back to Rhonda's truck and see if I can get a signal there."

A few minutes later Ron returned. "I managed to get hold of the local sheriff. Medical assistance is on its way. But I think it's too late for that."

"Did you film the actual moment when Rhonda was shot?" Samantha said.

"Yes. I was rolling."

"As gruesome as it is, the police will need to see that," Samantha said, still shaking. "I'll never be able to get that moment out of my mind. Who could have done this?"

"Someone who's a hell of a good shot,' Ron said.

***

Nadine was sitting in a chair on her front lawn, staring at the calm waters in the bay when Captain Davies called.

"I hope you're not too comfortable," Davies said. "We just received notice that a woman, Rhonda Quinlan, was shot dead near Katahdin while doing a TV interview."

"Is that the woman who planned on donating land to the park service?"

"The same. I guess she finally pissed off the wrong person," Davies said. "You'll be working with Sheriff Gastineau again on the case."

"I'm sure he'll be as helpful as ever," Nadine said.

"It is what it is," Davies said. "Just get up to Millinocket as soon as you can. Forensics has already dispatched a team."

Nadine made a call and booked a room at the Moosehead Lodge. Since she didn't know how long the investigation would last, she at least wanted to enjoy the rustic charms of the lodge once again.

12

"We meet again, Detective McAfee," Buck Gastineau said, grinning sarcastically. "I hope that you don't harbor any hard feelings."

"I don't harbor any feelings at all toward you," Nadine shot back. "Just stay out of my way."

"I'm just here to cooperate," Buck said.

"Did you know the victim?" Nadine asked.

"Yes. A local celebrity of a sort," Buck said.

Nadine walked over to the body of Rhonda, who had been placed in a body bag. Nadine unzipped the bag and stepped back in horror. It looked like Rhonda's head had exploded.

"Pretty nasty stuff," Buck noted, "Your forensics team found a shell casing a few hundred yards away, there in the woods. It's a 30-06 Winchester, probably fired by a Winchester rifle that's used for moose hunting."

"But there was not a moose here," Nadine noted wryly. "Where are the witnesses?"

"The PBS reporter and her camera operator are over there with one of the EMTs. The woman is pretty shaken up by what she saw," Buck said.

"I can only imagine," Nadine said.

Nadine walked over to the ambulance. An attractive young woman with blood spattered on her clothes sat on the bumper.

"I'm Detective McAfee. I'll be the lead investigator on the case. Are you injured? Tell me what you saw?"

"I'm not hurt. This is Rhonda's blood," Samantha said, beginning to cry.

"Just relax and tell me what happened and what you saw," Nadine said calmly.

"We had just completed the interview when I heard a shot, and then Rhonda was on the ground," Samantha said,

"You saw no one?"

"No," Samantha said.

"And you?" Nadine said, looking at Ron.

"I was filming the whole time. I have the actual moment when Rhonda was shot. Then I turned my camera towards the woods. I saw movement, but not a distinguishable figure, in the distance," Ron said.

"I'll need that digital file," Nadine said. "Maybe our team in Augusta can enhance the footage and make out something."

"Of course," Ron said.

After giving permission for the removal of Rhonda's body to the county morgue, Nadine crossed a field and entered the woods, where several members of the forensics team were combing the area.

"We found the shell casing. The sheriff, who arrived before you, knew immediately what type of bullet had been fired. We'll check for fingerprints when we get it back to the lab," the forensics lead explained.

"Did you find anything else, like cigarette butts or footprints?" Nadine said.

"Nothing. But if you follow me, we found a small dirt road where the shooter likely parked his vehicle and entered the woods."

Nadine walked through the dense woods until she came to a single-track dirt road that was only wide enough for an ATV.

"No truck or car could have navigated this road. It's too narrow and too rugged," the forensics lead said.

"I agree," Nadine said. "Can you get impressions of the tire tracks?"

"I believe we can."

"Finish up here and alert me as soon as possible about what you have found. I will also be sending you a digital video file that I'd like you to try to enhance," Nadine said.

Nadine looked for Buck Gastineau when she returned to the crime scene. She had received the contact information from Samantha and Ron; she informed them that they could leave.

"What are your thoughts about who could have done this?" Nadine said to Buck.

"You really want my opinion?" Buck said.

"Yes."

"The possible suspects are numerous. The consensus around here was that Rhonda Quinlan should have minded her own business. She should have never bought all of that land for her own political purposes," Buck said.

"Well, we have some evidence to go on: the shell casing and ATV tracks back in the woods."

"I don't know if that will narrow down your suspects. I own a moose-hunting rifle and an ATV."

"Did you kill Rhonda Quinlan?" Nadine said.

Buck laughed. "Even I draw the line at murder."

"I'll need to notify her family," Nadine said.

"She has a son who lives with her on her farm. His name is Damien. I heard rumors that she had another son from whom she had been estranged for years. Don't know his name or where he lives. Follow me, and I'll escort you to her farm."

Thirty-minutes later, Nadine knocked on the door of Rhonda's farmhouse. Buck had returned to the sheriff's office after having led Nadine to Rhonda's property. A man with a scruffy beard in his mid-thirties opened the door.

"Are you Damien Quinlan?"

"Yes."

"I'm Detective McAfee from Maine's Major Crimes Unit. I have some unfortunate news about your mother."

"I've been trying to reach her for hours on the phone," Damien said. "I figured she was out of range of cell service. What's going on?"

"I'm sorry to inform you that your mother has been shot and killed."

"What? She was supposed to be with a PBS crew doing an interview."

"She was. She was killed while with the crew,' Nadine said.

"Where?"

"On her land."

"I can't believe it," Damien said. "Who did this?"

"We don't have any suspects yet."

"Somebody had to know where she was to have killed her," Damien said.

Nadine agreed. This was not a random shooting or an accident. Someone had followed Rhonda and the news crew and waited for an opportunity to take a shot.

"I heard from Sheriff Gastineau that you have a brother. Is that true?"

"Yes. Darren. He's two years older than me. But we have had no contact with him in at least fifteen years. He went off into the woods somewhere and never reappeared. He could be dead. He could be living off of the land like a hermit," Damien said.

"And your father?"

"Died many years ago in a traffic accident," Damien said. "Where is mom's body?"

"At the county morgue."

"I need to go there and start making arrangements."

"I understand," Nadine said. "I'll be in touch with you throughout my investigation. I'm staying at the Moosehead Lodge."

Nadine returned to the lodge and awaited the findings of the forensics team. She needed to learn more about the missing brother. Was he dead, as Damien suspected? Or was he alive and had been harboring a grudge against his mother? A grudge that finally turned deadly.

13

Nadine read a 2015 *Vanity Fair* article about Rhonda Quinlan and her unconventional family history. Born into a Manhattan family that had made a fortune in cosmetics, Rhonda left New York for college at the University of California in Santa Cruz, where she studied environmental science. After earning her degree, she joined a commune located in the foothills of the Sierra Nevada Mountains, where she met Xander Beaumont, who would become the father of her two boys. She and Xander never married, Nadine learned.

Xander, Rhonda, and the two boys lived the communal life until the boys reached their teenage years. During their upbringing, the brothers were home schooled by their parents. Xander had a degree in biology from Stanford. It was during the time in the commune that Xander and Rhonda began experimenting with the low-tech production of a hand cream and soap that they sold at local farmers' markets in central California. The products became so popular that they became the primary source of income for the small commune of ten families. When the boys Damien and Darren reached college age, Rhonda wanted to leave the commune, which she had begun to feel was too insular and socially claustrophobic. The family of four moved back to New York City, where Rhonda took advantage of her family's business connections and started mass-scale manufacturing of the Nature's Balm product line. The business flourished. Damien began attending college at the Ivy League school Cornell University in upstate New York. Two years earlier, his older brother Darren had dropped out of Columbia University, saying that he wanted to travel. He was never seen or heard from again. Private investigators that Rhonda had hired believed that Darren was still alive, but was living off-grid in a remote and inaccessible enclave deep in the northern woods of Maine. There had been an alleged sighting of him as recently as five years ago, but then the trail went cold.

On a trip to pick up Damien from college, Xander was killed in a car accident. Even while grieving her partner's death, Rhonda's business continued to boom, making her very wealthy. She eventually decided to devote her life to conservation, which was always her first love, she told the *Vanity Fair* reporter. After selling the company, she and Damien moved to Maine and, over time, she accumulated the ninety-thousand acres of wilderness that she intended to donate to the nation.

Numerous conservative and right-wing groups had been attacking her character and motivations for years, but Rhonda had remained undaunted in her position.

After completing the article, Nadine felt a surge of admiration for this tough-minded and passionate woman who had been assassinated. She began her investigation by retracing Rhonda's movements in the days before she was killed. Damien mentioned that she had gone to a local hardware store to purchase fencing wire. Nadine visited the store and talked to the manager.

"Yes, I remember when she was here about a week ago," said Dale Smithers.

"Did she talk to anybody when she was here?" Nadine said.

"She exchanged a few words with a customer."

"Can you please be more specific about what happened?"

"She and this other guy got into an argument about her land. A lot of people around here are upset about what she was planning to do," Smithers said.

"Do you know the man with whom she was arguing?"

"Yeah. But it was really nothing. I don't want to get him into trouble."

"Rhonda Quinlan is dead. Somebody shot her in the head. So, I suggest that you cooperate with me," Nadine said forcefully.

"OK. His name is Howie Freed. He's a motorcycle salesman. He rides a big Harley. He works with his brother Hank," Smithers revealed.

"Is he a hunter?"

"Everyone around here hunts."

"Where can I find him?"

"On Lincoln Road. You can't miss the place."

Nadine drove along a dreary stretch of road that featured car dealerships, mattress outlets, and run-down convenience stores. She walked into a musty showroom jammed with a variety of motorcycles.

"I'm looking for Howie Freed," Nadine said.

"I'm his brother Hank. Howie isn't in today. Can I help you with something?"

"I'm Detective McAfee. I'm investigating the murder of Rhonda Quinlan."

"What's Howie have to do with that?"

"Just tell me where I can find him."

"I suspect he's hanging out with his buddies at The Broken Arrow, a local watering hole about a half-mile down the road," Hank said.

The Broken Arrow wasn't hard to find. Three motorcycles sat out front of a windowless wooden building. Coming inside from the bright summer sunlight, Nadine's eyes took a few seconds to adjust to the darkness of the bar that smelled like sweat and stale beer. Nadine saw two men playing pool and a third man at the bar chatting with the bartender. Every customer turned their head when Nadine waltzed in.

"I'm looking for Howie Freed," Nadine said in a booming voice.

"You don't have to yell," one of the men holding a pool cue said. "I'm Howie."

Nadine saw a man with a bushy beard and a shaved head. He wore a black tank top and jeans that looked a size too big.

"I'm Detective McAfee. Can we go outside to talk?"

"My brother just called, warning me that you'd be here. I've got nothing to say to you."

"I'll be the judge of that," Nadine shot back.

Howie placed his cue on the table and approached closely to Nadine.

"I said I have nothing to say to you," Howie repeated.

"What's a matter, Howard? Afraid to talk to a woman, Howard?" Nadine said, emphasizing the proper name of 'Howard' in a cutting tone.

Then the other men began a mocking chorus of "Howard. Howard."

"Hey, shut the fuck up!" Howie said. The men's laughter and chant quickly ceased.

Howie took another step closer to Nadine. At which point Nadine lunged for a pool cue and slammed it into Howie's groin. He groaned loudly and doubled-over, covering his crotch with his hands. When he tried to move toward Nadine again, she swung the pool cue like a baseball bat, hitting the side of his head with the full force of her swing, shattering the cue.

"Now, let's go outside and talk," Nadine said.

Howie submissively followed Nadine to the gravel parking lot.

"My head's bleeding," Howie said.

"You'll live," Nadine said. "Do you own a Winchester moose hunting rifle?"

"Yeah. So, what?

"Where were you around two o'clock yesterday afternoon?'

"In my apartment."

"Don't you ever go to work, Howard? I thought you worked for your brother. But you are claiming you were at home yesterday afternoon and today you're here drinking and playing pool. Sounds like a cushy job that you have," Nadine said.

"What do you want me to say? My brother gives me lots of leeway," Howie said.

"Do you own an ATV?"

"No."

"Do any of your friends own one that you borrow from time to time?"

"Yeah, sure.

"I'll need the names of those friends," Nadine said. "I heard you got into an argument with Rhonda Quinlan about a week ago."

"Yeah, she's just a rich bitch."

"But now she's dead."

"If you're thinking that I shot her, you're nuts. But I'm glad she's dead. I'll buy the guy a beer who did it."

"I'm going to get a search warrant for your apartment. You better be straight with me. Stop being a smart ass. This is serious. I'm a serious person, as you just found out inside," Nadine said.

"I didn't kill her. And I don't know who did," Howie said meekly.

"You can go. I'd wash the blood off of your face if I were you. You wouldn't want it to drip on the pool table," Nadine said.

***

The forensics team lead called Nadine at her hotel with two nuggets of relevant information. Howie Freed's gun had not been fired recently and could not be linked to the weapon that killed Rhonda. That didn't mean, however, that Howie couldn't have borrowed someone else's gun. But Nadine had her doubts that he was the killer. He seemed too lazy to have spied on Rhonda and then followed her to the woods on the day of the television interview. Forensics was also able to get a match on the tire treads that were found. They were from tires on a type of ATV called a John Deere Gator XUV. Nadine asked her team to find out how many ATVs of that brand had been sold in the entire state of Maine. It was a start, Nadine thought.

14

"Tell me more about your brother," Nadine said to Damien the day after Rhonda's ashes were scattered in the forest.

"He always loved the outdoors and was a bit of a recluse. Life in the commune suited him. But when the family moved back to Manhattan, he began to change. The crowds and the high-rise living didn't suit him. He became paranoid about everything. He began parroting conspiracy theories about big government taking away individual rights and putting dissenters in concentration camps," Damien explained. "After a couple of years of college, he told us one day that he wanted to get away. He packed up his camping gear and hopped on a bus at the Port Authority Bus Terminal. We have never seen or heard from him since."

"I read in an article that your parents hired private detectives to hunt for him. Is that correct?" Nadine said.

"Yes. The detectives reported hearing rumors about Darren living in the Maine woods near the border with Quebec. But no one ever had contact with him. Personally, I think the likelihood is that he's dead, and has been dead for a while. Either because he starved, had an accident, or was killed by another survivalist," Darren said.

"I'll need your mom's computer and phone. I need to check any correspondence she has had recently."

"Of course. I'll go get them for you," Damien said.

After Damien handed over Rhonda's electronic devices, Nadine asked Damien if Rhonda had been afraid of any person or group in particular.

"She received all kinds of threats, as you will no doubt find examples of on her phone and computer. But she never felt that her life was really in danger," Damien said.

"OK. Thanks for these materials," Nadine said.

"Oh, I almost forgot to mention that I received a call this morning from President Osgood's chief of staff. The president is going to announce the establishment of the Rhonda Quinlan Katahdin Wilderness Monument, which is the first step before a formal designation of a national park," Damien announced.

"That's great. Your mother prevailed after all," Nadine said.

"Too bad she isn't alive to see it, however."

As Nadine drove away from the Quinlan's farm, a pair of eyes followed her SUV until it vanished down the dirt track. Nadine and Damien had no idea that these same keen eyes, attuned to the most subtle movements of the forest, had been watching them the entire time.

***

"Are you sure that this list of registered ATV owners is correct?" Nadine said to the tech team lead.

"Yes. There are over two thousand ATVs registered in Penobscot County. But I think you'd be most interested in the names under the letter 'F'."

Nadine scanned through the Excel file and saw that an ATV of the type whose tracks were found on the trail belonged to Harold Freed.

"We already checked on him for you. He's the father of Howard and Henry Freed."

"This is great work. Thanks," Nadine said.

Nadine drove back to Hank Freed's motorcycle shop.

"What does your father do for a living?" Nadine said.

"He used to work at the old paper mill that's shuttered now. To supplement his pension and social security checks, he makes money as a guide. He takes locals and tourists hunting and fishing," Hank said.

"Does he own a John Deere ATV?"

"Yeah. So, what?"

"Your brother Howie failed to mention that when I spoke to him," Nadine said. "Where does your father live? I couldn't find an address for him other than this shop."

"He's not exactly the easiest person to find," Hank said.

"What does that mean?"

"He roams around in the woods, often times for weeks. Sometimes on foot. Sometimes on his ATV. He reappears from time to time to stock his provisions and to cash his pension and social security checks that are mailed here. He takes the occasional shower at my place," Hank said.

"When was the last time you saw him?"

"Must have been two or three weeks ago."

"Does he own a Winchester rifle?" Nadine said.

"Yeah, and dozens of other types of weapons."

"Do you think he could have shot Rhonda Quinlan?"

Hank hesitated to answer.

"If you know something, you damn well better tell me," Nadine growled.

"I don't know where he is or where he's been."

"Did he ever speak about Rhonda Quinlan?"

"Few people had much love for her around her, including my father," Hank said.

"Well, it appears Rhonda will get the last word from the grave. President Osgood has protected her land with an executive order," Nadine said.

"Who told you that?"

"Her son Damien."

"Fucking hell," Hank said. "Next the government will be taking our guns."

"I guess you better begin sleeping with them then," Nadine replied sarcastically.

Nadine was faced with the prospect of trying to hunt down a clear person of interest in Harold Freed, a skilled woodsman, in the vast Maine north woods. She knew that she didn't have the skills to undertake such a search on her own.

After returning to her room at Moosehead Lodge, she updated Captain Davies on the investigation.

"My prime suspect at this time is a skilled hunter and guide who could be anywhere," Nadine said. "But if anyone could have followed Rhonda's movement on the day of her TV interview and the days preceding it, Harold Freed would be that man."

"You've put me in a tough position," Davies said. "I don't want to assign officers to go on a wild goose chase through the woods."

"Can you wait a second? I'm getting an urgent text from Rhonda's son Damien," Nadine said, suspending the conversation. "Holy shit."

"What's going on?"

"I need to drop. Damien just texted me that his brother Darren, who no one has seen or heard from in fifteen years, has suddenly appeared. And that Darren knows who killed his mother and knows where to find him," Nadine said.

"What are you waiting for? Go!" Davis said.

Thirty minutes later Nadine pulled into the driveway in front of the Quinlan farmhouse. Standing on the front porch was Damien, and beside him a shorter man with a beard that reached to the midpoint of his chest. The man had long black hair that was tied in a pony tail. He wore ragged jeans, tan moccasins, and a tattered blue plaid shirt. Leaning against the porch screen was a rifle, a crossbow, and a quiver filled with homemade arrows. A docile black Lab lay at his feet with its head resting on its paws.

"Detective McAfee, this is my brother Darren," Damien said.

"Ready to go hunting?" Darren said.

15

"Is this the man you saw shoot your mother?" Nadine asked Darren while showing him a driver's license photo of Harold Freed.

"Yes. I was making my way down from the border with New Brunswick on very remote trails to make a surprise visit to see mom and Damien. I came across an old newspaper that somebody had thrown away. I saw an article about the land she was planning to donate. I wanted to see her. Fifteen years living alone in the woods can get to any person," Darren said. "Anyway, I had just walked onto mom's land when I heard a gunshot and then saw a burly man running through the woods carrying a rifle. He hopped on an ATV and rode down a muddy trail. My dog and I tracked him for an hour, but he had got gotten off of his vehicle and headed deep into the woods and across a stream. I think, though, that my dog Henry and I can find him again."

"Did you know at the time that he had shot your mother?" Nadine said.

"No. But I then returned to the place where I had initially spotted him; that's when I saw the police activity. Then I suspected it was mom who had been shot. And when I came here, Damien verified it for me."

"I'm sorry this happened," Nadine said. "Let me run back to my hotel and grab some gear. And then we can get started."

***

After alerting Captain Davies to her plans, Nadine drove back to the Quinlan farm, where she picked up Darren and his dog. She had stuffed her backpack with bug repellent, a rain jacket and pants, water, two bananas, a flashlight, and extra ammunition. She drove Darren to a trailhead in Rhonda's forest preserve, where they began their hunt for Harold Freed.

"What's your dog's name?" Nadine said.

"Henry. Named after Henry David Thoreau, who was my inspiration for how I lived the past fifteen years. About five years ago, I found the pup abandoned in a box on the side of a road. People can be so fucking cruel. He's been the only companion that I've ever had since I've been living off of the land."

"Where are we going exactly?"

"I suspect that Freed has a camp deep in the forest along the Abnaki River. It's secluded and has plenty of fresh water. Also, there's good hunting for deer. It's going to be a rugged slog, however."

"Let's just get on with it," Nadine said.

With the dog Henry leading the way, Nadine and Darren followed barely noticeable trails that wildlife used to navigate through the dense forest. The mosquitoes and black flies had begun to bite. The bug spray that Nadine had brought had little effect.

"Don't the bugs bother you?" Nadine said.

"I don't notice them," Darren said.

As they walked, Nadine observed how Darren glided effortlessly through the woods in his moccasins. He barely brushed a leaf or snapped a twig as he kept a brisk pace. Sweat began to stain Nadine's clothes as the heat and humidity rose. Fortunately, the dense tree cover protected them from the full intensity of the summer sun.

Through a break in the canopy, Nadine noticed Katahdin looming in the distance.

"Have you ever climbed it?" Darren asked.

"When I was younger," Nadine said.

"You should do it again."

"Have you got another pair of knees in your rucksack?" Nadine joked.

That comment made Darren laugh. It was the first time he had displayed any emotion besides silent determination. For a man who had lived in the wilderness for fifteen years, Nadine also noticed that Darren's teeth were in good shape. At least he practiced good oral hygiene, she thought.

After four hours of hiking non-stop, Nadine asked if they could take a break.

"We need to turn to the left at the big tree ahead," Darren said. "That trail will allow us to come up on Freed from behind. If we're lucky, we can make it there while there's still light. We've got the long summer days working for us."

The next trail on which they walked was more difficult as it featured many large boulders over which they had to scramble. The going was much slower, but not for Henry, who regularly turned around, tail wagging, waiting for the humans to catch up. After another three hours, Nadine heard the sound of rushing water.

"That's the Abnaki River. It's still running fast from the recent thunder storms," Darren said. "It's too dangerous to cross. That's why we came the way we did."

After another hundred yards, Darren stopped. He motioned for Henry to stop. The dog didn't move.

"I smell smoke," Darren said. "His camp must be close."

Nadine didn't smell anything.

Even though Darren carried a rifle, he placed an arrow in his crossbow.

"Here, you take the rifle," Darren said. "I prefer the bow."

"I have my Glock handgun," Nadine said.

"Take the rifle anyway," Darren insisted. "Let's split up and surprise him by coming in from both sides."

Nadine crept around to the right while Darren and Henry moved quietly to the left. Nadine then spotted the outlines of a tent, next to which a campfire smoldered. She saw no one. Darren must still be hidden in the woods, she said to herself.

Walking as softly as she could, Nadine approached the tent. The only sounds came from the rushing river, which had nearly topped its banks. Nadine took another step forward past a tree; then she was hit in the side of the head by the butt of a gun. Stunned, she could feel someone grabbing her by the hair and dragging her to the river. She screamed as a man threw her into the raging river. She was immediately assaulted by the cold water. She struggled against the fast current. She turned her head and caught a fleeting glimpse of a tall, barrel-chested man laughing at her on the bank.

On shore, the man heard a dog barking. He turned and fired a shot into the woods. Before he could aim and shoot again, an arrow plunged into his chest. He staggered backward. Another arrow sliced into him. He fell to the ground.

Darren saw what had happened to Nadine. He and Henry ran along the bank of the river, occasionally catching sight of her trying to keep her head above water. A few hundred yards downstream, Nadine managed to grab hold of a fallen tree limb, which stopped her momentum. Shivering and coughing up water, she saw Darren and Henry arrive, just when she had thought she would soon die in the frigid river.

Darren pulled a rope out of his backpack and yelled to Nadine.

"Grab hold of this!"

Darren tossed the rope toward Nadine several times, but she couldn't reach it with her right hand. On the third attempt, she finally clutched the rope. Darren pulled her to the river bank.

Drenched and bruised from striking the river rocks, Nadine lay exhausted in a bed of pine needles.

"What about Freed?"

"He's dead," Darren said.

***

Since Nadine couldn't get a cell phone signal, Darren and Nadine spent the night at Freed's remote camp. Nadine slept in Freed's tent, which smelled like tobacco and dirty clothes. Darren and Henry slept outside, with Freed's corpse laying nearby. Darren had covered the body with a blanket.

The following day Nadine, after hiking out with Darren and Henry, informed Captain Davies about what had happened and where she was. It was another two days before Freed's corpse could be extracted by a rescue team.

After completing her final report proving that Harold Freed's gun had fired the shot that killed Rhonda, Nadine sat with the reunited brothers on the porch of Damien's homestead on a cool summer night.

"Do you plan on hanging around?" Nadine asked Darren, who had trimmed his beard and cut his hair. She could now better see his resemblance to his brother.

"Damien and I have talked about it. We have a lot to catch up on. And we both want to work on preserving mom's legacy," Darren said. "Plus, even though this place has the creature comforts that I never experienced, or frankly missed, for all of those years, it is still remote enough for my taste."

"I do need help to look after the place," Damien said.

"I think Henry here likes sleeping by the big fireplace at night. He's settled in nicely," Darren said. "What's next for you?"

"I never know," Nadine said. "For now, I'm going to return to my house in Porcupine Haven. That's my special place that soothes me.

"We all need such a place," Darren said.

PART 3: NEIGHBORS

16

"I have a job for you," Matt Volansky's agent Tim Robarts said.

"What time is it?" Matt said groggily.

"It's nearly noon your time. It's morning here in L.A.," Tim said.

"Shit. I have a class to teach in an hour," said Matt, who was an adjunct professor of creative writing at the University of Maine in Orono. His college friend Cody Hendricks, a biology professor at the university, had helped him secure the position when Matt's screenwriting work had dried up.

"Make your pitch quick. What's the gig?" said Matt, rising from bed. He lived in a small two-bedroom rental house not far from campus. He looked outside and saw barren trees swaying in the early November breeze. He sensed that snow was lurking somewhere near the Canadian border.

"Have you heard about the best-selling thriller called *Death Watch*?" Tim said.

"No. Should I have?"

"It's already sold five-million copies. The movie producer, Vince Bergman, is a fan of your early screenplays, especially *A Lovely Way to Die* and *In a Dark Place*. He considers them classics."

"Because they are," Matt said.

"Well, he called me wondering if you were still alive. He thought you had died about ten years ago."

"In a sense I had," Matt said.

"When I told him that you were alive and relatively well, he offered you the first crack at adapting the novel for the big screen. It will be, at minimum, a six-figure paycheck," Tim said.

"Can you send me the book? I want to actually read it before I commit to adapting it," Matt said.

"I'll overnight a copy to you."

"OK. I really have to go now. It's my day to shape young minds."

"God forbid," Tim said.

Matt looked at himself in the mirror of his bathroom. His face was gaunt and his hairline had retreated. Not unusual for man who just turned fifty, he thought. He still tried to run a few miles every day, but with the weather turning colder, he knew that he was about to be forced inside for many months of Maine hibernation, a perfect time to sit down to write a screenplay for which he might actually receive a writer's credit and a hefty paycheck. For the past ten years, he'd been supplementing his modest teaching income with ghostwriting work on several low-budget, straight-to-streaming movies and various cop dramas on TV.

This semester, he was only teaching one course: The Art of the Thriller. He was barely able to pay his rent with the stipend from just that course. But he didn't mind. The college town of Orono kept him away from the many vices he had in Los Angeles, namely needy women and needier booze. He was grateful that his college buddy had lobbied to get him the teaching work. Over the years, he had made some friends with other members of the faculty. And he exchanged superficial chatter with his neighbors on the block; they considered him a celebrity of sorts. If they only knew, he mused.

Even though he owned an old Honda SUV, Matt decided to walk to campus on this day. As he exited his house, his neighbor Sharon Woodbridge appeared in her driveway. Sharon was an emergency room nurse at the local hospital. Matt had always found her attractive. He and Sharon had flirted on a few occasions across their shared backyard fence.

"Coming home from your night shift?" Matt said.

"Yes. Very busy tonight. One heart attack and a motorcycle accident," Sharon said.

"In contrast, I did nothing," Matt joked. "I have to get to class."

"Let's catch up later. Maybe a drink?"

"Only in moderation," said Matt before picking up his pace and heading to campus a half-mile away.

***

Vicky Sturgis had taken one other writing class from Matt. She had shown herself to be a good writer. She wrote crackling dialogue and had a flair for crafting the unforeseen plot twist. Vicky was also very attractive. A volleyball player, she was tall with powerful shoulders.

As promised by Tim, Matt had received a copy of *Death Watch*. The novel weighed in at over five hundred pages. When he removed it from the mailing enveloped, he sighed. He didn't want to waste his time reading through such a long book. He didn't have the patience.

He asked Vicky to stay after class.

"Have you read this book?" Matt said, pointing to the paperback sitting on his desk.

"Yeah. It's great," Vicky said. "It would make a great movie."

"It just so happens that I have an opportunity to write the screenplay. But I'm really busy. Would you mind re-reading the book and writing out for me a plot summary and a character analysis? I'd pay you."

"I'll do it for free just for the chance to work with you," Vicky replied excitedly.

"You don't mind? You have the time?"

"I'll make the time," Vicky said enthusiastically.

"That would be great," Matt said. "By the way, there's this big guy lurking by the door and peering in from time to time."

"That's my boyfriend Brandon. He's very impatient."

"Well, you better not keep him waiting."

***

Sharon looked out of her window and saw a tall woman entering Matt's house. Since they had chatted in her driveway the week before, Sharon had on several occasions invited Matt over for a drink. But he declined, claiming he was working on a new project. Sharon wondered if the new project was bedding this lanky undergraduate.

Sharon noticed a black Jeep Wrangler slowly cruising past her house and then stopping briefly in front of Matt's house on one of the days when Sharon knew the young woman was with Matt. Sharon wondered if the vehicle contained the woman's boyfriend. Or it could be a burglar looking for empty homes to rob, she thought.

She kept staring out of her window at Matt's house. From time to time she would see two figures in silhouette behind drawn curtains. She continued to monitor Matt's house until it was time for her to head to the hospital for the beginning of her shift at midnight.

17

Joyce Vance was an early riser. She lived outside of Orono on a small two-acre plot located off of a main road. She and her husband, now deceased, raised their brood of four children in their comfortable home. Now her primary companions were her two golden retrievers: Holly and Honey. Joyce walked her dogs on a cold November morning. Frost encased the ground. Her feet crunched on the dead grass as she and the dogs followed their familiar path into the woods from the backyard of the house.

After about a half-mile, the forest intersected with a narrow gravel road. The dogs were the first ones to see the twisted figure that had been tossed along the side of the road. Joyce cautiously walked toward the body of a tall woman whose neck appeared to be twisted at an unnatural angle.

"You poor girl," Joyce whispered before saying a silent prayer. She then called the police.

***

"Do we have an ID?" Nadine said when she arrived at the crime scene outside of Orono.

"Yes," said a member of the forensics team. "Her name is Vicky Sturgis. She's a student at the university."

"Cause of death?"

"Broken neck. She also has bruises and scrapes consistent with being thrown from a vehicle."

"Time of death?"

"I would say sometime between midnight and four or five in the morning."

"Did you find anything else?" said Nadine. "Was there a sexual assault?"

"Nothing. My guess is that she was killed somewhere else and dumped here. No evidence of rape. But the medical examiner will have to confirm that."

"Get her body to the medical examiner so we can get a toxicology report and a more detailed post-mortem examination," Nadine said. "I'm heading to the university."

Being on campus again brought back fond memories for Nadine. She had enjoyed her four years at the University of Maine. But, as she walked among the buildings, she also thought that so much had changed in her life. The friends she thought she would have forever had drifted away and started their own lives. Many of them had families now. No one would have thought that she would be investigating murders and sometimes shooting people in self-defense. The walk to the campus's administration building had suddenly turned melancholy.

"I'm Detective McAfee. I'd like to speak to the university president about one of the students. It's urgent," Nadine said.

"Have a seat please," the friendly administrative assistant said.

A few minutes later, Nadine was ushered into the office of Lillian Fentriss, the university's president.

"My assistant said that there's been an incident involving one of our students," Fentriss said.

"Yes. I'm sorry to tell you that Vicky Sturgis has been found dead. She's been murdered," Nadine revealed.

"That's awful. I can't believe it," Fentriss said. "Do you know who her killed her?"

"No. I've just begun the investigation. I need to know where she lived and what her daily schedule was."

"Of course. I'll get that information to you immediately."

"Can you do me a favor and contact her parents?" Nadine said. "I think it would be more appropriate for them to learn the news from you. The parents can contact the state medical examiner's office in Augusta, where Vicky's body has been sent for further examination."

"Of course. Please keep me informed about your investigation."

"I will," Nadine said.

***

The off-campus apartment where Vicky lived with two other female roommates was very familiar to Nadine; she had lived in the same complex during her junior and senior years with her friend Sara Goodwin. Nadine took the roommates by surprise when she knocked on their door and then introduced herself to the women named Cindy and Kelly.

"What's going on?" Cindy asked.

"When was the last time you saw Vicky?" Nadine said.

"Last night around seven o'clock I'd say. She said she was going out to work on a class project," Cindy said.

"But you weren't alarmed when she didn't return this morning?" Nadine said.

"No. We figured she spent the night at her boyfriend Brandon's place," Kelly volunteered. "Will you tell us what this is all about?"

"Vicky was found dead along the side of a road earlier this morning. She had been murdered."

As soon as the word 'murdered' had flown from Nadine's lips, the women began to cry. Nadine stood silently and let the women take in this shattering information about their friend.

"You mentioned a school project. For what class was this?" Nadine said.

"Vicky was taking a screenwriting class with this teacher named Mr. Volansky. She told us he was once a big shot in Hollywood. She was working with him on some screenplay," Cindy explained.

"Do you think that she was having an affair with him?"

"No. She and Brandon have been dating since she was a freshman," Cindy said.

"But you don't know for sure?"

"Well, I guess not for sure."

"Were there any problems between Brandon and Vicky? Did she ever say if he hit her or verbally abuse her?"

"No. Nothing like that," Kelly said. "But he always wanted to know where she was. Vicky did find that annoying. You don't think Brandon killed her, do you?"

"I'm not accusing anybody," Nadine said.

"I'm sending a forensics team here to look through Vicky's room and take her computer. Please cooperate with them when they arrive later this morning," Nadine said.

While sitting in her car, Nadine Googled Matt Volansky. She saw that he had quite an impressive record of screenwriting accomplishments, at least up until a decade ago when his creative juices apparently had run dry. She found his number in the university's faculty directory.

"Is this Matt Volansky?"

"Yes. Who is this?"

"I'm Detective McAfee. I'm just five minutes away from your house. I'd like to talk to you about Vicky Sturgis."

"About Vicky? Why?"

"I'll be right there," Nadine said.

Nadine knocked on the door of Matt's house. She noticed a Honda SUV in the driveway.

"You must be the detective. Come in," Matt said. "Now, what's this about?"

"When was the last time you saw Vicky Sturgis?"

"She was here last night. She left shortly before midnight."

"She left alone?"

"Yes."

"Can anyone verify that?"

Matt thought for a moment. "Yes. My next-door neighbor Sharon. She's a nurse who works nights. She was just coming out of her house when I was saying goodnight to Vicky," Matt said. "Go ask her."

"I will," Nadine said.

"And you never spoke to Vicky after she left?"

"No. Will you please tell me what's going on?"

"Vicky Sturgis is dead. Murdered."

"Fucking hell," Matt said.

"I talked to her roommates. They told me she was working with you on some project."

"I got this contract, my first big one in years, to write an adaptation of the best-selling thriller called *Death Watch*. I asked her to help me get my head around the main plot lines and characters of the book, which is massively long," Matt said.

"And that was the entire nature of your relationship?"

"Was I screwing her? No. Look at me. I'm an old man who sometimes drinks too much. She would only humiliate me if I even tried to come on to her. I'm not that vain or self-confident to think she'd be interested in sleeping with me," Matt said.

"It's good to hear that you know your limitations," Nadine said. "Did she ever talk about her boyfriend?"

"Not really. I knew she had one. A big guy. That's about all I know."

"No one picked her up when she left here?"

"No. Her apartment is really close," Matt said. "It was a nice night. She decided to walk. It's safe around here. Or so I thought. There's really not anything more I can say."

"Then you wouldn't object to a team searching your car or your house?"

"Go ahead," Matt said. "Now, I must get to class. I guess I'll have to tell them about Vicky. And then I'll cancel the class for the day."

Nadine then walked over to Sharon's house. She rang the doorbell and a woman in her thirties still wearing her pajamas answered the door.

"Sorry to wake you," Nadine said, "I'm Detective McAfee. Your neighbor Mr. Volansky said that you saw him with a young woman last night. Is that correct?"

"Yes. I was heading out the door to begin my night shift at the hospital. I'm an ER nurse. The woman was just leaving."

"And what time was that?"

"Sometime before midnight," Sharon said. "Maybe eleven thirty. Why do you ask?"

"The woman was found murdered this morning."

"My god. That's terrible. You don't think Matt killed her, do you?"

"I'm just trying at establish a timeline," Nadine said. "Thanks for your time."

After Sharon saw that Nadine had departed, she called Matt, inviting him over for dinner that night.

"It'll do you good to talk to someone about what happened to your student," Sharon said.

18

"I never saw Vicky the night that she was killed," said Brandon Jennings.

"Where were you then?" Nadine said.

"I was here in my apartment with my roommate Kyle. He can verify that."

"Did you talk to her at all that night?"

"Yes. She called me before she went to meet her teacher at his house. She said she would walk home to her apartment after she was done working. I also texted her during the night, but I received no response. You can check on all of this," Brandon said.

"I will," Nadine said. "How did you feel about your girlfriend spending so much time with her teacher?"

"I didn't like it. There was something creepy about Volansky. I don't know what it was," Brandon said.

"Did Vicky have any concerns about him?"

"No. She thought he was this great writer who would help her. She wanted to write movies like he did. That's all she talked about," Brandon said.

"Where is your roommate Kyle, by the way?"

"He's at hockey practice. He and I are teammates. But I blew out my knee working out during the summer. So that's why I'm not with him," Brandon explained.

"Give me Kyle's cell number. I need to speak to him directly to verify your alibi," Nadine said.

After leaving Brandon's apartment, Nadine thought to herself that Brandon was certainly capable of easily strangling a woman. He was well over six-feet tall with a muscular upper body and large hands. But if indeed he was at his apartment, he didn't kill Vicky.

***

"What was it like living in L.A.?" Sharon whispered to Matt as they lay together in bed. It hadn't taken long for dinner to turn to drinking and then to sex.

"It was fun, lucrative, surreal, and ultimately damaging all in equal measure," Matt said. "Yes, I met celebrities. I went to some wild parties. But I was always anxious, wondering what my next project would be. And if I could score another hit. At the end of the day, Hollywood is a company town like Detroit. Lots of people just doing their jobs to get a product out of the door."

"And what about the women? You never married?" Sharon said.

"I lived with this aspiring actress named Cecile for five years. She did the occasional commercial, but she never landed any TV or movie roles, even minor ones. That led to her depression and drug taking. I couldn't take it anymore, so I kicked her out."

"What happened to her?"

"She went back home to Utah. Never heard from her again," Matt said. "What about you? Why are you still single?"

"I work long hours and see a lot of misery," Sharon said. "It takes a lot out of me. At the end of the day, I don't want to have to be a supportive girlfriend or wife. I just want to decompress. I want to get away from people mostly."

"But yet here you are with me," Matt said.

"I think we're kindred spirits. I've kept my eye on you since you moved next door. There's a worldliness in your eyes that I find alluring."

"You find me alluring?" Matt laughed. "You have been spending too much time around broken bones and blood."

"You write about thugs, killers, and other deviant people. I've watched most of the movies you've worked on. You are able to dredge up the worst of people in your plots," Sharon said.

"It's not that hard. There's a killer inside everyone," Matt said.

"You really believe that?"

"People are capable of all sorts of evil. But most of us have something called a conscience that checks us," Matt said.

"Could you kill me?"

"Under the right circumstances. And you could kill me also."

Sharon turned on her back, her breasts pointing upward.

"Get on top of me and put your hands around my neck," Sharon demanded.

"Come on, Sharon. I can think of more pleasurable things that I can do with my hands."

"Just do it!" Sharon yelled. "Just for a few seconds."

"OK," Matt said reluctantly.

Matt placed his hands around Sharon's neck and began tightening his grip. As the force of his grip increased, Sharon wrapped her legs around his thighs. She kept her brown eyes open as he squeezed. Then Matt let go. Sharon let out a sigh of pleasure. Then she grabbed his crotch hard with her right hand.

"I've got an hour before I have to go to work. Let's make the most of it," said Sharon.

***

"Your roommate Brandon told me he was at the apartment all night. But Vicky was killed in the early morning hours. Were you up all night?" Nadine said.

"We both went to bed late, after midnight. He was hoping that Vicky would come over. But she didn't," Kyle said.

"You didn't hear Brandon leave the apartment?"

"No. I would have heard the door close."

"But you're not absolutely certain that Brandon was in his room all night?"

"He wouldn't have killed Vicky. He had no reason to," Kyle said.

"Did you ever see them fight?"

"All couples fight."

"Did he ever tell you that he hit her?"

"No. Just because we are athletes and play a violent sport doesn't mean we are violent people. We leave that stuff on the ice," Kyle said defensively.

After speaking to Brandon and Kyle, Nadine wasn't ready to dismiss Brandon as a suspect. But she was less convinced than before that Brandon was the killer. Could Vicky have had a random encounter with stranger that went terribly wrong? Anything could have happened in the three blocks from Volansky's house to her apartment, Nadine thought.

***

As Sharon rose naked from bed and walked to the shower, she informed Matt that he could stay the night in her bed and let himself out in the morning. Matt demurred, telling her that he wanted to return to his house and continue working on the screenplay. Matt suddenly felt a rush of energy, a feeling that he thought had forever eluded him. After he departed Sharon's house, he sat in front of his computer until dawn, writing feverishly. He occasionally looked at the detailed notes that Vicky had prepared for him. She had been a huge help in getting him started on this project that he now believed would usher in a renaissance to his career. Too bad Vicky was dead, he thought; she deserved a thank you.

19

Tim Robarts recognized his client Matt's creative skills, but he didn't trust Matt's diligence. There had been too many deadlines missed in the past; too many angry outbursts at studio executives; too many times when Matt had walked away from a deal because he had become bored. This time Tim would not be taking any chances. He decided to travel to Maine to check personally on Matt's progress on the screenplay.

After a full day of airline travel from L.A., Tim arrived at Matt's modest dwelling in Orono.

"Not quite like the house you once had in Malibu," Tim said.

"That was a lifetime ago," Matt said. "This abode suits me fine."

"Can I see what you've done so far?"

"Of course. I've nearly completed the first draft," Matt said, pleased with himself.

Matt handed over a huge pile of paper to Tim, who was surprised at the sheer volume of pages.

"I know *Death Watch* was a long read. But your job was to condense it into a two-hour screenplay, not a TV miniseries," Tim said.

"Just read it and let me know what you think," Matt said. "I have the guest room fixed up for you. You have the house to yourself while I'm on campus today. And my friend Sharon will be joining us for dinner," Matt said.

"Is it getting serious with her?" Tim said.

"I don't know if I can really be serious about anyone," Matt replied.

After Matt departed to teach his university class, Tim settled down in the living room to read Matt's screenplay. The sky began to spit snow. After just twenty pages, Tim realized that Matt had digressed from the book's plot. He even had invented a new suspect in the murders that were at the core of the book. The meticulous detective who was the hero of the story had been turned into a boorish womanizer. The studio and the dedicated readers of a bestselling book didn't want Matt Volansky's take on the book; they wanted a faithful adaptation. This was not it, Tim thought.

Tim fretted for the rest of the afternoon until Matt returned. He entered the house with the attractive neighbor Sharon. Because of Sharon's presence, Tim held his tongue while she prepared dinner. The trio then engaged in a benign conversation for two hours over steaks and wine. Tim noticed that Sharon kept up with Matt's intake of wine glass for glass. Before sobriety had flown out of the window, Tim decided to bring up the subject of the screenplay.

"I spent the afternoon reading your work so far," Tim said.

"Isn't it great?" Sharon chimed in. "Matt let me read it. I think it's some of his best work."

"It certainly has some chilling moments," Tim said.

"One of my students, the young woman who was killed, helped me get started. I wish that she was here to share in the credit. She had some good ideas that I incorporated into the plot," Matt confessed

"You see, Matt, the thing is: what you have written so far doesn't align with what the novelist wrote," Tim said.

"That novelist can't write worth shit. What I did was incorporate elements from the great tradition of film noir. It now has a darker texture, and more complicated characters with tortured souls," Matt said.

"But it's not what you were commissioned to produce."

"This will be better."

"I don't think the studio will agree with that assessment."

"Fuck the studio," Matt said, his voice rising. "Convince them that audiences will love my treatment of the book."

"I'm not going to do that," Tim said.

Matt then arose from the table with a wine bottle in his hand. He swung, hitting Tim flush in the left side of his skull, knocking from the chair in which he was sitting to the floor. A huge cut had opened up, causing blood to drip onto Tim's blue Oxford shirt.

"Matt, stop it!" Sharon yelled. She went over to Tim and helped him up. She pressed a napkin to his head to stem the flow of blood.

"You're going to need stitches. And the swelling has already started," Sharon observed. "Let me drive you to the emergency room. My shift is about to start anyway."

"Tim, I'm . . ." Matt began to speak.

"Don't say a fucking word to me," Tim spat out.

On the drive to the hospital, Sharon asked Tim if he had ever seen Matt act like that before.

"Yes," Tim revealed. "He has a violent streak. He can lash out at anyone at any time. I thought he had his temper and drinking under control. But he usually calms down after one of these episodes."

"We're almost at the hospital," Sharon said. "We'll get you fixed up and then you can take a cab back to Matt's, if that's where you want to go."

"He just apologized to me in a text," Tim said, looking up from his phone. "He's on his way to the ER. He'll take me back to his place once I've been checked out."

"OK. You know him better than I do," Sharon said.

***

"We just arrested a burglary suspect whom I think you might be interested in," Buck Gastineau said to Nadine.

"Why is that?"

"We caught him prowling around the neighborhood where Vicky Sturgis was last seen. This guy says he has some information. He wants to deal on the burglary charge."

"He just could be bullshitting you," Nadine said.

"Maybe. But do you have any leads yet?" Buck said.

"Point taken. Where is he now?"

"We've got him locked up in the county jail."

"I'll be right over," Nadine said, surprised that Sheriff Gastineau was being so cooperative. She wondered what he was really after.

Curtis Wright had a pockmarked face and eyes like a weasel. He was sniffling and rubbing his nose when Nadine walked into the interview room. Nadine hoped that he wouldn't sneeze on her.

"I'm Detective McAfee. I hear from the sheriff that you like to steal other people's things," Nadine said.

"Maybe," Curtis said, wiping his hand across his nose.

"What did you see three nights ago on Ingersall Street?"

"I was cruising the neighborhood. I then parked at the corner of Ingersall and Strand. I saw this girl walking alone. Then this guy comes up behind her. He pulls at her jacket. I couldn't hear what they were saying. But it didn't look like a friendly conversation. Then she goes back down the street with this guy," Curtis recounted.

"Describe the girl."

"Look, it was midnight. It was dark. But this girl was tall and had light hair. I can tell you that."

"And the other person?"

"Shorter. He wore a black hoodie and maybe dark blue or black jeans and white tennis shoes. That's all I could see. I didn't see a face."

"What did you do then?"

"I'm not saying anything else until I speak to my lawyer."

"You didn't kill that girl, did you, Curtis? Maybe you decided to upgrade your criminal profile from burglary to murder," Nadine said.

"I didn't touch her. Check my car. You won't find any evidence there linking me to that girl. I don't kill people."

"You just rob them."

"It's what I'm good at," Curtis said, flashing a wry smile.

After the interview with Curtis had been completed, Buck asked Nadine if she thought Curtis could have killed Vicky Sturgis. Buck wondered if Curtis was making up the whole story about the encounter that he claimed to have witnessed to negotiate a plea deal.

"I actually believe that he witnessed something," Nadine said. "But I don't think he's the killer. I do need to follow up on what he told me." Nadine then called Matt Volansky, telling him that she needed to speak with him again.

20

"What happened here?" Nadine said as she greeted Matt and Tim at Matt's house.

"It's nothing," Tim said. "I had a fall after I had too much to drink."

"You didn't bandage that wound yourself. It looks professionally done. You went to the ER, didn't you?" Nadine said.

"My neighbor Sharon, whom you met, took Tim here to the hospital out of an abundance of caution," Matt said.

"And you are?" Nadine said, looking at Tim.

"Tim Robarts. I'm Matt's agent. I came here to review a project that Matt is working on." Tim said.

"Matt, I need you to come to the station for another interview. New evidence has come to my attention regarding Vicky Sturgis," Nadine said.

"What do you mean?"

"We'll discuss it at the station."

"Matt, do I need to call a lawyer to represent you?" Tim said.

"No. I'll cooperate with Detective McAfee. I have nothing to hide. We'll continue our discussion when I get back," Matt said.

On the short drive from Matt's house to the police station in Orono, Nadine asked Matt what he was referring to with Tim.

"Tim and I need to work out our differences about this script that I've been working on," Matt said.

"The one you and Vicky were working on you mean?"

"The same. It's typical Hollywood back and forth."

After arriving at the station, Nadine escorted Matt into a small interview room.

"Matt, you have some secrets," Nadine said.

"I don't know what you mean."

"I checked your record. You've had multiple alcohol-related driving arrests in California. You were arrested twice on domestic violence charges, but the woman named Cecile eventually refused to testify. You seem to like assaulting women, Matt. Is that what you did to Vicky Sturgis, and things got out of control?"

"I told you she left my house by herself and I never saw her again. My neighbor Sharon corroborated that. You said so yourself," Matt said, growing anxious.

"But I now have a witness who observed a person approaching Vicky on the street near your house. The witness saw the person arguing with Vicky and then the two of them left together," Nadine said. "Was that you, Matt?"

"No. Absolutely not. It could have been anyone."

"This person wore a black hoodie and dark jeans with white tennis shoes. If I searched your house and your trash, would I find them there, Matt?"

"You already searched my house and car for evidence. And you found nothing. I didn't see Vicky again after she left. I didn't talk to her again," Matt insisted.

"I'm going to have your house searched again, just for the fun of it. Do I have your cooperation? Or do I need to get a warrant?" Nadine said.

"I have nothing to hide. Search away," Matt said.

Nadine stepped out of the interview room to make a call to the forensics team.

"A team will be here to search your property again in two hours. Until then, I'd like you to remain here," Nadine said.

"Am I under arrest?"

"No. But I don't entirely trust you, Matt."

Nadine met the forensics team at Matt's house. Nadine asked Tim Robarts to find someplace to be until the search had been completed. Tim said that he would find a coffee shop in which to get some work done.

"There's a nice place just two blocks from here," Nadine said. "You can walk there."

"Where's Matt?"

"I left him at the station so he can contemplate the situation he's in."

"Is he in trouble?"

"I'll know shortly," Nadine said.

Nadine and two members of the forensics team conducted a more thorough search of Matt's property, from the basement to the attic.

"Detective McAfee, I think I found something," a team member yelled.

Stuffed in the bottom of a cardboard box in the closet of Matt's bedroom was a men's large black hoodie.

"This hoodie was stuffed beneath a pile of old manuscripts. We also found a pair of white tennis shoes and several pairs of jeans colored both dark blue and black."

"Good job," Nadine said.

Nadine encountered Tim as he was returning from the coffee shop. Tim noticed that Nadine carried several items of clothing in evidence bags.

"What's going on?" Tim asked.

"I suggest that you get a lawyer for your friend Matt. I'm going to charge him with murder," Nadine said.

"That's crazy. Matt wouldn't kill anyone."

"Well, this time the dead body wasn't just on the page of one of his movie scripts," Nadine said.

***

Within twenty-four hours of his arrest, Matt was back at his house, out on bail, courtesy of the quick work of Clyde Trainer, the studio lawyer whom Tim had contacted. Clyde had flown overnight to arrive in Maine to secure Matt's release.

"Do you own that black hoodie that the police found?" Clyde asked.

"I never saw it before in my life," Matt said. "I'm not a hoodie kind of guy."

"Yet, it was hidden in a box in your bedroom closet. How do you explain that?" Clyde said.

"Someone must have broken in while I was away. Someone's trying to frame me. Maybe it's Vicky's boyfriend," Matt said. "She told me that he could be jealous."

"The police looked at him. They can't connect him to the murder," Clyde said. "If you did have anything to do with the woman's death, maybe it was an accident. Maybe I can get the charge reduced in a plea deal. But you need to tell me the truth."

"I didn't kill her," Matt said confidently. "Look, the police took a DNA sample after they arrested me, right?"

"Yes."

"They're not going to find my DNA on that hoodie because I never wore it," Matt said. "They won't find any matches from me or from Vicky."

"You're positive?"

"Yes. Absolutely."

"Let me talk to the lead detective and the district attorney to see where things stand," Clyde said.

***

After arranging for Matt's defense counsel, Tim Robarts returned to Los Angeles. He had to tell the movie producer for *Death Watch* to find another screenwriter. He also wasn't certain that Matt was telling him the truth. He believed that Matt was capable of murder and knowing how to cover it up. He shared these feelings directly with Matt before he departed Orono.

Stung by Tim's lack of belief in his innocence, Matt visited Sharon, who suggested that they get out of town and breathe in the fresh air out in the woods. Matt agreed, not because he especially liked being outdoors in frigid weather, but because he liked being with Sharon.

"It's fucking freezing today," Matt said, walking beside Sharon in the forest.

"I know how we can warm things up," Sharon replied provocatively, while pressing her body against Matt's.

"You've got to be kidding," Matt said, pushing her away.

Sharon slapped Matt across the face and then, with a grip that surprised him, wrapped her forearm around his neck and began choking him.

"Let go, you crazy bitch!" Matt said, struggling to release her grip. He bit part of her arm, but she didn't flinch.

"Is that what I am? Would you rather be fucking Vicky?"

"I never did anything with her," Matt said, gasping for air.

"This is how she died, you know, struggling to breathe, just like you are now. She pleaded for her life in the backyard of my house. I knew what you and she had done. I saw the two of you through the window," Sharon said. "Don't take me for a fool. That night, I followed her on the street. I told her that you had sent me to bring her back to your house; that you wanted to work with her just a little longer. She willingly walked back with me towards your house. I strangled her behind my house, and then I dumped her body along the side of the road."

"And you were wearing a black hoodie, weren't you?" Matt said.

"You catch on quickly. You should write movies," Sharon hissed. "No one betrays me. I demand loyalty."

"I didn't betray you," Matt said. "You're the one who framed me."

"I had to do it, Matt. I'm in control. I've always been in control!" Sharon yelled, as she choked the life out of Matt.

After Matt had slumped to the ground, Sharon walked to her car, and then returned with a length of rope that she secured around Matt's neck. She tossed the other end of the rope over a thick tree limb and pulled Matt's limp body upwards, until it dangled above the ground. She was surprised at how little he weighed. Then she secured the other end of the rope to the tree trunk. To complete the vignette of a suicide by hanging, Sharon carefully piled large stones near Matt's feet to show that he had built a small platform which he then kicked aside before he hanged himself. Satisfied with her work, Sharon removed her gloves and drove back to her house.

***

"My client claims that he didn't own the black hoodie that you found," Clyde said to Nadine. "You won't find any of his DNA on it. I think you need to turn your attention to Vicky Sturgis's boyfriend."

"You are right. We didn't find any evidence that Matt had worn this hoodie. Yet it was hidden in his house," Nadine said.

"Somebody planted it there," Clyde said.

"Don't tell me that you're one of those conspiracy theory types," Nadine said.

There was a knock on the door. "Detective McAfee, I'm sorry to interrupt. But we have a report of a body being found in the woods about a mile out of town. It's Matt Volansky. He's dead. It looks like he hanged himself," the officer said. "We also have a witness who was walking her dog. She saw a man and a woman walking together in the woods. Then the witness saw just the woman driving away alone about thirty minutes later."

***

Nadine looked at Matt hanging from the tree. His dead eyes bulged from his head, now tilted at an unnatural angle.

"Get him down," Nadine told the responding officer.

"Isn't he the guy you suspect killed that college student?" the officer said.

"I don't suspect him anymore," Nadine said.

Nadine drove immediately to the hospital and asked if the ER entrance had security camera footage. The hospital administrator confirmed that the facility did have security cameras at each employee and public entrance. Nadine asked to see the footage from the night of Vicky Sturgis's murder. At the timestamp of one o'clock in the morning, Nadine spotted Sharon Woodbridge entering the hospital. Sharon wore a black hoodie, dark jeans, and white tennis shoes.

21

State police and county sheriff's units searched for Sharon Woodbridge. Several alleged sightings turned out to be false alarms. When officers searched Sharon's house, they found a trove of adult sexual bondage toys. The lady liked to inflict pain, Nadine thought.

Twenty-four hours after the search had begun, there was still no sign of Sharon or her vehicle. Exhausted, Nadine returned to the Moosehead Lodge. As she stepped out of her SUV, a figure jumped on her from behind, wrapping an arm around her neck and bending her torso backwards.

Nadine used her upper-body strength to pry loose the arm that was trying to strangle her. Once free, she turned and saw Sharon, who began to run through the parking lot into the forest.

Before giving chase, Nadine checked that her gun had not been dislodged during the struggle with Sharon. There was no moon. Nadine's eyes had not fully adjusted to the darkness as she pursued Sharon. But she could hear Sharon's footsteps ahead, crunching on the dead fallen leaves on the forest floor. Slowly, Nadine's eyes had adjusted enough to the darkness to discern Sharon running ahead of her, darting from tree to tree. Then Sharon disappeared. She must have jumped into a ravine, Nadine thought.

Nadine slowed her pace, taking the Glock out of its holster. She moved forward cautiously. A rock hit her square in the forehead, knocking her backward. She saw Sharon running toward the bank of the Penobscot River. There was nowhere for Sharon to go, unless she tried to cross it. With her forehead dripping blood into her eyes, Nadine caught up with Sharon. She pointed her gun at her, telling her to get down on her knees and turn around.

"It's over, Sharon," Nadine said, catching her breath.

"Vicky and Matt deserved to die. They wanted to be together. Now they are, in a way," Sharon said.

Nadine couldn't help but think of the contradiction that a woman who worked to ease people's pain in the ER could be so callous and vicious towards people in her private life.

"Get on your stomach and put your hands behind your back," Nadine ordered.

"I usually don't mind being restrained. But not under these circumstances," Sharon said.

"Just do what I say."

"I don't plan to spend any time in a prison cell," Sharon said.

Sharon then sprinted to the river and jumped in. The current swept her away into the darkness. Nadine didn't even hear her scream. There was only the sound of the water rushing over the glacial rocks.

***

Nadine learned that Sharon Woodbridge's corpse was found the following morning. But she had more pressing issues to think about. After returning to her room at the lodge, she received a call that her grandmother Martha had suffered another stroke and was unresponsive. Nadine rushed to the hospital in Waterville, where Martha lay unconscious and on life support.

"I'm her granddaughter," Nadine told the attending physician. "I have the power of attorney."

"I don't think she's going to wake up," the doctor said. "The stroke was massive."

Nadine stroked Martha's gray hair and held her hand. Nadine's heart told her that there was some life in those wrinkled hands. But her head told her that Martha really wasn't there any longer.

"There's really no chance that she will wake up?" Nadine said.

"In my opinion, no," the doctor said calmly.

"Then I think it's time to let her go. She's lived a long life," Nadine said. She turned her face away from the doctor so that he wouldn't see her crying.

***

After the funeral service, Nadine donated what few belongings Martha still possessed to various charities. The only items that Nadine kept were Martha's beloved recipe books. Back at her house in Porcupine Haven, Nadine made a batch of Martha's famous chocolate chip cookies.

She had invited her old college friend Sara Goodwin to spend the weekend with her. When the cookies came out of the oven, the women each took a cookie in one hand and a glass of chardonnay in the other and toasted the woman who had raised Nadine.

"Here's to the wisest and kindest woman I've ever known," Nadine said. "May she rest in peace. And may I live up to her ideals."

PART 4: FAMILY GHOSTS

22

His colleagues at the University of Iowa were surprised when Drake Halsey, at the age of only fifty-five, decided to resign his tenured teaching position and move to the north woods of Maine to live in the house that his father, who had died at the age of eighty, had left him in his will. The chair of the English Department suggested that he should just sell the house and the fifty acres that sat on the edge of Baxter State Park in the shadow of Mount Katahdin. But Drake could not bring himself to do that. Drake had grown weary of teaching undergraduates and decided, along with his second wife, the poet Eleanor "Ellie" Kurtz, to try to make a living from his modest early retirement pension and free-lance writing assignments.

Drake and Ellie sold their house in Iowa City and drove cross-country to the log-cabin that Drake's father had built for the family as a summer retreat nearly fifty years ago. Drake's father had inherited the land from his father. Drake felt a special familial connection to the remote site. It was his legacy. His only sibling, his older sister Grace, had died last year. Therefore, he was the only member of the Halsey family who was still breathing. Drake fondly remembered spending summers at the house, where his father Roland wrote his popular historical novels when he was not hiking through the forest and climbing the slopes of Katahdin.

Drake and Ellie were both poets. Drake had been awarded the Pulitzer Prize four years ago and Ellie, twenty years his junior, was considered to be one of the fresh new poetic voices in the country. Ellie, however, was often in fragile health. Drake hoped that fresh air and vigorous exercise would improve her physical condition. He had told friends that, at times, he had grown weary of nursing his sickly wife. "I'm twenty years older than her, and I never even get a cold," he boasted. "But she seems to be always sick or on the cusp of some malady."

Before his death, Roland Halsey had entrusted the care of the property to his nearest neighbor Russ Tanner, a gruff former logger. Drake and Ellie stopped at Russ's homestead to retrieve the keys for the house and to receive a report from Russ.

"I kept everything locked. And I checked on the house every few days since your father's funeral," Russ said. "Even though it's pretty remote out here, I didn't want hunters and hikers coming upon an empty house, breaking in, and then ransacking it."

"I appreciate that, Russ," Drake said.

"Are you ready for this?" Russ said. "I remember you and your sister coming here since you were kids. But now you have to take care of the place. You won't have the cushy life you once had."

"We know that, Russ. We're ready," Drake said.

"Well, I'm an old man, but if you need anything, you know where to find me. And if you find me dead one day, just dig a hole and toss me in it," Russ said.

"That would seem like a fitting send off," Drake joked. That comment caused Russ to laugh.

Ellie had not seen the property since the funeral for Drake's father three months ago. When she arrived at the cabin this time, it looked smaller. The property also looked more desolate and darker because the summer run barely filtered through the thick canopy of trees.

"Well, here goes," Drake said, opening the front door.

A musty smell greeted the couple as they walked into the house, which featured a large living area that had a screened-in porch in the back overlooking a small pond. Next to the living room was a kitchen and a small bathroom. Drake had explained to Ellie that the house did have running water, fed by a nearby fresh-water spring, and electricity powered by a gas generator.

"My mother wouldn't have lived here without some basic amenities," Drake explained.

Up a narrow set of stairs were three bedrooms. Drake and Ellie would use one in which to sleep. The other two would be converted into their respective libraries and studies.

Ellie opened all of the windows to invite fresh air into the rooms. When she opened a kitchen cabinet, a mouse sprang out and disappeared in a corner.

"You'll have to get used to sharing these confines with forest creatures from time to time. There's no way to avoid them, I'm afraid," Drake said apologetically.

Drake had one more place to show Ellie. He opened a small door at the back of the kitchen. He turned on a flashlight and led Ellie into a small basement with stone walls. The space was barely high enough for either one of them to stand.

"This is the cellar that dad built by hand. We can use it to store food all year around," Drake said.

"Good to know," Ellie said as she scraped a spider web from her hair.

Drake and Ellie began the laborious task of emptying their rented U-Haul trailer of the possessions that they had brought from Iowa. Since the cabin was furnished, they just brought with them their clothes, books, and other items of sentimental value. Drake, who was tall and lanky with thinning brown hair, hoped to rebuild his muscles with rigorous physical exercise. He had regaled Ellie with tales of his wood-chopping prowess when he was a boy. But the sedentary nature of academia had withered his upper body.

Ellie, in contrast, was small; barely five feet in stature. But she possessed shapely legs, penetrating green eyes, long fingers, and sandy brown hair. She was prone to bouts of pneumonia and bronchitis, however, which could sap her strength and vigor for weeks at a time. Before the move to Maine, Drake assured her that there were adequate medical services in Millinocket if she needed them.

After spending the better part of the July day emptying the trailer, Drake grilled the two of them chicken for dinner. They sat on the porch sharing a bottle of wine and marveling that the sky was still light at nearly ten o'clock at night.

Exhausted, they fell into bed an hour later. Ellie, however, was restless. She kept hearing creaks and moans that unnerved her. Because it was so dark in the house, she dared not venture out of the bedroom for fear that she would run into something. She thought she heard a woman breathing heavily. Could it be her own respiration? Drake lay next to her sleeping comfortably. Ellie decided that she was imagining things. Well after midnight, she finally closed her eyes and fell asleep. She didn't notice that a mouse had crawled over her face as she dreamed.

23

A week after they had arrived at their cabin, Drake and Ellie had settled into their routine of spending most of their day sequestered in their respective offices working on their poetry. But to be able to make money, Drake in particular, given his status, had to be in contact with the outside world. This wasn't easy in such a remote location. But he installed a satellite dish that enabled phone and internet service, which he used to remain in contact with editors and publishers in New York. He landed a job as editor of a twentieth-first century poetry anthology, and he began a series of articles for the *New Yorker* about rural life in Maine's north woods.

Ellie, however, quickly began to struggle with the living conditions. She had only written one volume of poetry, which had received praise but scant sales. She always had hovered in the shadow of Drake. This didn't bother her as much when she had a group of supportive friends around her back in Iowa City, but here in the woods she had no one. Her days were filled with anxiety over not producing verse; her nights were filled with trepidation at the sounds she thought she heard coming from the dark recesses of the cabin.

Looking again at another piece of blank paper, she decided to go for a walk.   Drake warned her to be careful since she wasn't familiar with the acreage around the cabin. Ellie chose a path that began at the edge of the pond and then headed gently upwards into the woods. After thirty minutes, Ellie began to breathe heavily. She muttered to herself about her damn fragile lungs. Shortly after catching her breath, she heard a sound behind her. She was afraid it was a bear or a moose. But it was neither.

Emerging from the woods was an old woman with a stooped frame. Her gray hair hung loose to the middle of her back. She wore a ragged flower-patterned dress and ankle-high hiking boots. Her face was shriveled like a pumpkin that had been left outside for too long.

"You startled me," Ellie said. "I thought you might be a bear."

"Bears won't bother you. It's moose that you have to be afraid of."

"Good to know," Ellie said. "My name's Ellie. My husband Drake and I moved into the cabin back there."

"I know," said the woman. "I know everything that goes on around here."

"What's your name?" Ellie said.

"Cleo," the woman said. "Short for Cleopatra."

"That's an unusual name. But a nice one. I've never met a Cleopatra."

"Well, now you have. But call me Cleo. I live a few miles north. Between your cabin and Russ Tanner's."

"How long have you lived in the woods?"

"All my life," Cleo said. "My mother was a wild child who fled New York City shortly after I was born. She never told me who my father was. I assume he was of no account. She found an old cabin that she fixed up. She grew vegetables and hunted. And she worked from time to time as a waitress at a little restaurant in Millinocket. But she's dead now."

"How did you go to school?"

"My mom taught me everything I needed to know to survive out here," Cleo said. "I get by."

"I'm having a hard time getting used to the nighttime sounds. I keep hearing voices and footsteps when there are neither," Ellie said.

"I knew your husband's mother Nancy. She had a hard time out here also. Roland wasn't a very nice man. He was a strange man. I remember your husband Drake. He was a strange boy. A cruel boy. Like his father. I know what went on at that cabin. But I kept my mouth shut," Cleo said.

"What do you mean?"

"Ask Drake about his mother," Cleo teased.

"She died of a heart attack when Drake was a teenager," Ellie said.

"Did she? And ask Drake about the missing hikers," Cleo said. "Maybe it's their voices that you hear."

"I better be getting back to the cabin," Ellie said. She wasn't sure if the old woman was dangerous, or just crazy. But she didn't want to remain in her presence any longer.

"Come by my place anytime. I'll show you how the forest provides," Cleo said. "And take care of yourself. I could hear you breathing yards away. Lung trouble, I suspect."

Ellie walked back to the cabin, confused and a little frightened about her unexpected conversation with Cleo. She wasn't sure she wanted to tell Drake about her encounter. During dinner, Drake discussed his work for the day. He read aloud a first draft of his poem about climbing Katahdin. Ellie thought that the poem was very evocative.

"I need to get you up on Katahdin one of these days," Drake said.

"I don't know if my lungs could take it," Ellie said.

"You need to strengthen them. Living out here will be the best thing for you. Sometimes I grow tired of being your caretaker and your husband," Drake said coldly.

Taken slightly aback by Drake's comment, Ellie decided to change the subject.

"I ran into an old woman named Cleopatra, of all things," Ellie suddenly interjected. "She looked like one of those fairytale witches."

"Cleo is still alive? She must be in her eighties by now. When I was a little boy, her mother was still alive. She and her mother used to waltz through the woods naked back in the day," Drake revealed.

"That must have been quite a sight for a little boy," Ellie said.

"I was more amused than titillated," Drake said. "What did the two of you talk about?"

"Not much. But she did mention a story about missing hikers. Does that ring a bell?"

"That's been a mystery that swirled around these parts since I was a boy. A group of three hikers, two men and a woman, got lost in an early autumn snow storm back forty years ago now. Their bodies were never found. Some people said they were murdered. But the police figured their bones were somewhere out in the woods," Drake said. "They likely died from hypothermia. So, if you stumble upon their remains, you'll become a local celebrity."

"That's not the way I want to attract attention," Ellie said. "Do you hear strange sounds at night?"

"No. I sleep like a dead man when I here. You know that. I guess I'm used to all of the nocturnal creaks and groans that this old place has. Don't let it bother you," Drake said.

"I'm not sure if I'll ever get used to it," Ellie said.

24

Ellie tried to put off going climbing on the rock-strewn slopes of Katahdin for as long as possible. She first claimed that she was focused on writing a long poem and she didn't want to break her creative flow. Then she said she was feeling ill. But after each excuse, she could tell that Drake was becoming increasingly annoyed. His yelling increased in intensity. He had always been so calm and controlled. But since arriving at the cabin, he had become more short-tempered. Finally, Ellie relented.

Drake drove them to Baxter State Park, where they checked in at the ranger station, and began hiking on the

Saddle Trail, which Drake said was the easiest for beginners. Flies and mosquitoes began biting as Drake and Ellie started walking through the first part of the trail to Chimney Pond, where they rested. Ellie's breathing was heavy, but she had survived so far. Drake gently encouraged her to continue.

The next part of the hike involved scrambling over boulders to the summit. There was no level ground. Ellie's ankles began to hurt. She told Drake that she couldn't continue.

"We've come pretty far," Ellie said. "Can we turn back now?"

"We've barely begun the climb. We can't stop now," Drake demanded.

"What differences does it make?"

"It tells me how resilient you are. If you're cut out for living here," Drake said sharply.

"This is not a test," Ellie shot back.

"Isn't it? Don't do to me what my mom did to dad. Don't become a liability out here," Drake snapped. "But if you insist, we can turn back. But I have to tell you that I'm very disappointed."

Ellie did not respond. The couple returned to the trailhead without speaking to each other.

When they arrived back at the cabin, Drake went into his study and closed the door. Ellie grabbed a bottle of wine from the refrigerator and sat in a chair by their pond until the sun had set and the bottle was empty. Then she took a hot bath to soothe her aching body.

Later that night, Ellie once again had trouble sleeping. With Drake slumbering next to her, she grabbed a flashlight from the nightstand and descended the stairs to the kitchen. She stopped and listened. She thought she heard footsteps in the cellar below. But she knew that could not be. She thought about waking Drake up and having him check. It was probably some creature that was roaming around down there. But since Drake was in such a sour mood, Ellie decided to investigate the cellar on her own.

She climbed down the narrow wooden steps. Since there was no railing, she placed her hand on the cool stones to maintain her balance. The bright beam of light caught the flash of a mouse running into a crack in one of the stones. In the far corner, Ellie noticed that one stone high up in the wall had become dislodged. At first, she was afraid that some animal might be using the crevice as a nest. She maneuvered the light into the hole. To her relief, there was no animal there. But she did notice that an object had been crammed into the cavity. She cautiously placed her hand in the hole. She pulled out a book with a leather cover. It was a diary written by Drake's mother Nancy. A cursory glance at the dates revealed to Ellie that the entries were made during one six-month period nearly forty years ago, the year in which she died.

Ellie was unsure of what to do. Her first inclination was to awaken Drake and show the diary to him. But her curiosity got the best of her. She returned from the cellar with the diary and placed it in her desk. Then she went back to bed.

The following morning Drake appeared to be in a better mood. Ellie asked Drake again about the lost hikers.

"Were you here when they went missing forty years ago?" Ellie asked.

"Yes, it was in early September, just before I headed off to boarding school at Exeter. The weather was pleasant, and then it turned nasty. I remember the wind howling and the trees snapping under the weight of the unexpected snowfall. The temperature dropped well below freezing. Without proper clothing, the hikers had little chance of survival," Drake said.

"Was there a search party organized?" Ellie said.

"Of course. In fact, dad and Russ Tanner joined the search. But the bodies were never found," Drake said.

"Wasn't that about the time your mom also died suddenly?"

"That's right. I wasn't here at the time. But dad told me and my sister, who was still alive then, that mom just fell over. A heart attack. He didn't even bother taking her to the hospital. He knew what had happened, he later told me," Drake explained.

"Where is she buried?"

"Somewhere on this land."

"What? She wasn't given a proper funeral or burial? What about her side of the family?"

"Dad never got along with her relatives. After she died, he alerted them, of course. But by then, she was already dead and buried. He didn't believe in religious services. He just returned her to the land."

"So, he never divulged even to you where he buried your mother?" Ellie said.

"No. And I never asked. I think it's better that I don't know. She is everywhere and nowhere. I like that idea," Drake said, who then announced that it was time for him to get to work. Ellie knew that meant she would not see him again until mid-afternoon.

Ellie retreated to her study and began reading Nancy's diary entries from forty years ago. It soon became clear to

Ellie that Nancy was being physically abused by Drake's father Roland. Nancy described in harrowing detail being beaten for not preparing dinner the way Roland liked it. As the summer of 1980 continued, Nancy's abuse at the hands of her husband continued. Then Nancy wrote about a freak autumn storm and the search for the lost hikers. Ellie had to prevent herself from gasping when she finished reading those pages. She started shaking violently. She carefully hid the diary in the back of the closet of her study. She then walked past Drake's study. His door remained closed.

Ellie walked outside into the forest. She wasn't sure how long she had wandered. She smelled smoke, and then she came upon the cabin when Cleo lived. Cleo was outside washing clothes in a large metal cauldron under which a wood fired burned to heat the water.

"I know what happened to those lost hikers," Ellie told Cleo. "And you do, too."

"Come inside. We'll talk," Cleo said. "I'll brew us some tea."

Cleo's cabin was dark but surprisingly neat to Ellie's eye. She expected that Cleo would be a hoarder. But the main room was immaculately maintained. And on the far wall was a generously stocked bookcase.

"I found Nancy Halsey's diary hidden in the cellar of the cabin. It's true, isn't it?" Ellie said.

"Yes."

"Yet you didn't say or do anything."

"I wanted to keep alive," Cleo said.

"But now we have to alert the police," Ellie said.

"We don't have to do anything."

"But I can't live with Drake now that I have this knowledge."

"You won't live long if he discovers that you know the secrets from his past," Cleo warned.

"You don't think he would. . ."

"I know he would," Cleo said, cutting Ellie off. "Go back to the cabin. Burn that diary and live to see another dawn."

"You need to help me," Ellie begged. "Come with me and we'll confront Drake together."

"I'm an old woman," Cleo said.

"But a tough one," Ellie said.

25

"We received an anonymous tip about a case from forty years ago," Captain Davies informed Nadine.

"What is it about?"

"You were too young to remember. Hell, I don't think you were even born yet. But up near Millinocket, three hikers went missing. Their bodies were never recovered. Now, all of these years later, we get a call out of the blue that someone thinks they know where the bodies are," Davies said. "And the caller said they didn't die a natural death. They had been murdered."

"I assume you want me to lead the investigation?" Nadine said.

"That's right. I've dispatched a team up there with the general location that the caller provided us."

"This may be a gigantic waste of time and personnel," Nadine warned.

"Maybe. But we need to follow up on it. There would be a shit storm if word got out that we didn't search for their remains."

Nadine drove from her home in Porcupine Haven to Millinocket, where she again checked into the Moosehead Lodge. The owner greeted her warmly upon her return.

"What brings you back here, Detective McAfee?" manager Doris Charles said. "I haven't read about any murders in the area."

"Do you remember an episode from a long time ago about three hikers who went missing?"

"Oh, yes. A terrible tragedy. They got lost in a freak autumn storm as I recall," Doris said. "Likely froze to death."

"Well, maybe not. That's what I'm here to investigate."

"Oh, that sounds exciting," Doris said.

After settling into her room, Nadine contacted the forensics lead, who gave her the directions to the location where they would be searching for three graves.

"We've received permission from the owner, a woman named Ellie Kurtz, to search her property."

Nadine made the drive through twisting and desolate dirt roads until she came to a staging area, where the forensics crew had been waiting.

"The anonymous caller said the place we should search was in a ravine near the bend of Flint Creek," Nadine said. "So, let's get started."

Nadine and the crew slogged through dense forest for over a mile until they reached the designated location.

"This is certainly a long way from any of the hiking trails on or near Katahdin," Nadine said, looking at a detailed map of the area. "How and why did they even make it here? And who would know about it?"

"I don't know. My job is to dig," the forensics lead replied.

Three hours of digging had turned up nothing. While taking a lunch break, Nadine noticed two women coming towards the site.

"Excuse me," Nadine yelled. "You have to stay away. This is a secure site. You didn't notice the yellow police tape?"

"Here in the north woods, we don't recognize boundaries," the older woman said.

"And who are you?"

"I'm Cleo. And this is my friend and neighbor Ellie," Cleo said.

"This is your land?" Nadine said to Ellie.

"Yes. My husband Drake and I own the property. But it's been in Drake's family for decades," Ellie explained.

"Yes. Now I remember your name being mentioned," Nadine said. "Nevertheless, you have to stay away and let us do our work."

"Of course, we were just out for our daily stroll. Cleo is teaching me about all of the medicinal qualities of the various trees and plants in the forest," Ellie said.

"That's a good thing to know if you live way out here, I guess," Nadine said. "But we really have to return to work."

"Of course," Ellie said. Then she and Cleo disappeared into the dense forest.

With the afternoon shadows lengthening, one of the team members yelled: "I've got something here."

A few minutes more careful digging revealed a skull and then an entire skeleton. By nightfall, two more skeletons had been found.

"There's a bullet hole in the back of each skull. These people had all been executed," the forensics lead said.

"These aren't just bones. They were human beings: Jill Hunt, Roger Avery, and Chet Wakeman," Nadine said.

***

When Ellie and Cleo had returned to Ellie's cabin, they went into the cellar to check on Drake, whom they had secured to a chair with rope. They had gagged his mouth with an old dish rag. Ellie pulled the rag out of his mouth. Drake screamed.

"No one can hear you," Cleo said.

"My hands are killing me," Drake said. "I need medical attention. An infection will set in."

Ellie looked down at Drake's right hand, which now was missing the two fingers that Cleo had cut off with a hunting knife to persuade Drake to tell them the entire story about what had really happened to the three hikers and his mother. Drake confessed that his father had abused his mother for years. One day, when Drake's older sister was away at college, Drake saw his father punch his mother so hard that her head snapped back. Then he strangled her right in front of Drake.

"You didn't see a thing," Roland screamed at his teenage son, according to Drake's account. "We both know what happened to those hikers. This is our secret for life. Your mother died of a heart attack. That's the new family history that we are writing together and from which we will never waver. Your life depends on you never telling anyone what you just witnessed."

Drake confessed to Ellie and Cleo that he was so afraid that his father would kill him that he did whatever his father ordered him to do. He then explained that Roland burned Nancy's body and placed her ashes in the wall of the cellar. He and his father never knew about the diary she had kept that told of her abuse and of the murder of the three hikers.

It was only after Cleo had amputated a second digit from Drake's right hand that he filled in the details about the hikers' deaths.

"My dad, mom, and I were hunkered down here in the storm when we heard shouting outside," Drake recalled while his three-fingered hand dripped blood on the cellar's dirt floor. "We were surprised when we saw the three frozen hikers. We invited them in to sit by the fire and ride out the storm. The young woman named Jill was very attractive. I was still a virgin and dad knew it. He took me aside and whispered to me. He told me we could both have her. Then he went upstairs for a moment, returning with a handgun. He shot the two men in the head right as they sat by the fire. In horror, mom watched the whole grisly episode transpire. Then we took the woman upstairs and, you know."

"You and your dad both raped her," Ellie said. "And then shot her."

"Yes," Drake said. "Then after stripping them and burning all of their clothes. We carried their bodies to a ravine near Flint Creek, where we buried them. I don't know why, but I insisted that we bury them instead of burning them. I felt it was the right thing to do."

"A fucking noble gesture," Cleo barked at Drake.

After Drake had told Cleo and Ellie this sordid family tale, Ellie made the anonymous call to the state police.

"How could you have kept such an awful secret your entire life?" Ellie said.

"Because it was so awful," Drake said, wincing in pain. "And I was afraid. I was weak."

"And what would you have done to me if you had discovered that I had found the diary?" Ellie said.

"Isn't that obvious? I would have protected myself and my father's legacy," Drake said.

"You disgust me," Ellie said.

"Are you going to turn me over to the police?"

Ellie and Cleo looked at each other. They smiled. Ellie placed the gag back into Drake's mouth. They left him sitting in the dark and dampness of the cellar. They waited for nightfall.

26

Nadine was astonished after listening to Ellie explain the tragic saga of the three hikers and how they died a brutal death forty years ago. She sat in Cleo's cabin with Cleo and Ellie.

"Was it you who made the anonymous call?" Nadine said.

"Yes. I had accidentally discovered Drake's mother's diary that chronicled all of the heinous acts that he and his father committed all of those years ago," Ellie explained. "After my encounter with you yesterday, I returned to the cabin. I pleaded with Drake to confess to the police what had happened. I was even willing to go along with his story that his father was totally responsible for the hikers' murders and that he had nothing to do with it."

"How did he react to that?" Nadine said.

"The bruises that you see on my face were his answer. He threatened to kill me. I was able to get away in the middle of the night and run here to Cleo's cabin. We kept a watch all night with a loaded gun. But Drake never showed up to threaten us," Ellie said.

"I dispatched two officers to your cabin. It was empty. Drake must have fled. Does he know these woods well?" asked Nadine.

"Even though he might appear to be this eccentric professor and poet, Drake has outdoor skills. After all, he spent years living here. He knows how to hide and survive in the wilderness," Ellie said. "At least for a while."

"Well, be could not have gotten far. He just had a few hours head start. The state police and county sheriff are already organizing a search party. We'll find him soon enough," Nadine said confidently. "Does he own a weapon?"

"He has a deer hunting rifle," Ellie said.

"Good to know. I'll send out an alert that Drake Halsey is armed and dangerous," Nadine said. "Are you sure you don't want to see a doctor about your injuries?"

"I'm fine, thanks," Ellie said. "I'll stay with Cleo tonight before returning to my cabin. Don't forget the diary. I assume that you'll need it as evidence."

"Yes. Thanks," Nadine said, taking the diary from Ellie's hands.

After Nadine had departed Cleo's cabin, Cleo and Ellie smiled at each other.

"The bruises on my face were a nice touch," Ellie said. "But you didn't have to hit me so hard."

"I had to make it believable," Cleo said. "They'll fade soon enough."

***

After a week with no signs of Drake Halsey, the intensive search was called off. But he was still a wanted man. Authorities thought that he had either died in the wilderness or was being harbored by a sympathetic neighbor. Russ Tanner was considered someone who might be protecting Drake. But after lengthy questioning by Nadine and an extensive search of his property, no signs of Drake were found. "Now that I know what he and his father did, I wouldn't protect that son-of-a-bitch rapist and murderer," Tanner said to the police and to reporter Emily Cooper of the *Bangor Beacon.*

Emily wrote obituaries of the victims Jill Hunt, Roger Avery, and Chet Wakeman. She also interviewed their closest living relatives. She tried unsuccessfully on multiple occasions, however, to secure interviews with Ellie and Cleo, but both women declined. By the end of the summer, few people talked anymore about the bodies that had been found. Life and the news cycle had moved on. Nadine suspected that a hunter would find Drake's remains in a few months or maybe a few years. But she was convinced that he was dead.

***

After the hysteria had died down, Ellie resumed her routine at the cabin. She had decided to stay in the woods in the shadow of Katahdin. She had received a lucrative offer to write a memoir and to take over the editing of the poetry anthology that Drake had started. When she was not hunkered down writing, she continued to wander in the woods, sometimes alone and sometimes with Cleo, with whom she had developed a deep and abiding friendship.

She no longer had trouble sleeping. She had adjusted to the rhythms of the forest and the change of seasons. But on certain nights when the air was still and the moonlight filtered through the trees, she would venture down to the cellar, pull a stone out of the wall and hold in her hands a small glass container. She stared at the fine gray granules sitting in the container.

"Thank you, Drake," she said. "I would not have had all of this if you hadn't pushed me out of my comfort zone."

PART 5: NORTH WOODS NOIR

27

Sam Rockland sat behind home plate watching the Portland Sea Dogs play on a warm August evening. Although he was enjoying the game against their opponent from Scranton, he was also there to observe the movements of a woman called Mona Crowell, whose husband had hired him to follow her. She sat two rows in front of him, accompanied by a man who was not her husband. Sam took out his cell phone and snapped photos of the adulterous pair. After the game, he followed them to a hotel by the wharf. The photos, the hotel liaison, and the text messages that he had hacked would be enough for his client, a trucking company executive, to file for divorce and contest the prenuptial agreement, since Mona was clearly violating its terms.

This was not the kind of work that Sam preferred. He found it sleazy and mildly depressing. He considered himself a security expert, but work had been slow at his company called Black Diamond, so he took whatever work came his way to pay the bills. Former high-profile clients from the worlds of entertainment, sports, and business often asked him why he was based in Portland, Maine. He told them that he wanted to operate inconspicuously. But truth he told, he was born in Maine and liked it. After serving in the Special Forces on multiple tours of duty in Iraq and Afghanistan, he returned to Maine to start his security firm. He offered personal protective services to well-heeled individuals whose financial assets put them or their families at risk from kidnapping, extortion, or possibly murder.

After preparing his report for Mona's soon-to-be ex-husband, he returned to his house that he was in the midst of remodeling. Unmarried and not looking for a spouse, he spent his time breaking down walls, repainting, and reflooring his Cape Cod-style house about a mile from Portland's bustling downtown business district.

His clients were often surprised when they first met him. He was thin and almost professorial in appearance. He had a smooth face framed by auburn hair. He preferred to keep in shape by bicycling rather than by jacking up his muscles in the gym. He was fluent in Arabic as well as the romance languages of Spanish and French, whose literature he regularly read in its original, untranslated form.

He was painting the newly plastered walls of his study when he received a call from one of his clients: Dirk Atwater, who owned an international shipping company and who had two children: Sybil and Paul. Sybil was the eldest. A graduate of the London School of Economics, she was being groomed by her father to take over the company.

"Sybil was staying at her home in a gated community in the Hudson Valley when she was awakened by breaking glass," Dirk said. "She ran into her safe room and closed the door. She stayed there for over an hour before the local security company she hired to monitor the house arrived and let her out."

"Was anything stolen from the house?" Sam asked.

"Nothing. I think Sybil was the target. It could have been a kidnapping attempt," Dirk said.

"Possibly. But it could have been just a routine robbery. I wouldn't assume that it was a kidnapping," Sam said.

"Whatever the motive, the incident unsettled Sybil. I want her to get away for a while. And I want to hire you to look after her," Dirk said.

"You want me to come to New York?" Sam said.

"Actually, no. Our family owns a large swath of land in the north woods west of Millinocket. We have a small stake in a logging company, but the rest of the forest we use for recreation. We have a comfortable house there. It's very secluded. I'd like Sybil to hunker down there for a while," Dirk said. "The seclusion will calm her nerves. She gets rattled easily."

"And your daughter is OK with this plan?"

"I'll tell her that she has no choice," Dirk said. "She'll be arriving in Portland by plane tomorrow. From there you will drive her to the house. My assistant will email you the directions."

"It sounds like you have everything thought out," Sam said.

"You are one of the best. Just keep my daughter safe," Dirk said.

"That's one thing I'm good at," Sam said.

***

In addition to being an executive vice president at Atwater Shipping, Sybil also funded a grass roots political organization focused on ending racial discrimination and economic injustice, particularly as experienced by America's indigenous peoples. As an undergraduate at Duke University, she wrote a master's thesis on the forced removal of tribes from their ancestral lands in the Great Plains. That research fired her desire to support the tribes' efforts in whatever way she could. And she had the deep pockets to do so.

She had been monitoring and supporting a protest by members of the Sioux nation against a proposed natural gas development near their reservation in South Dakota. Her father Dirk looked disapprovingly on her support for the tribal organization, which he believed was too radical for a business executive to be involved with. But Sybil persisted despite her father's objections.

Before the break-in at her home, however, she received the type of publicity that her father warned her might come her way. During the fortieth day of a standoff at the proposed gas plant, a member of a local right-wing white militia was found tied with barbed wire to a fence post and scalped. He had been shot four times through the chest. The local police in South Dakota had no suspects, but the murder raised suspicions among the militia group that a member of the tribe had been the killer. The situation on the ground was tense. The local and national media quickly seized on the fact that Sybil Atwater was the tribal organization's chief financial benefactor.

"We run a business," Dirk scolded Sybil in front of her brother Paul, who served on the company's board and who ran a small division of the firm that focused on cargo shipping in the Great Lakes. "We're not a bunch of radicals."

"They're not radicals. They're trying to protect their land from yet another unlawful seizure by corporate interests, and the white man," Sybil shot back.

"I want the Atwater name to be associated with shipping, not riots, murders, or unlawful insurrections," Dirk replied.

Sam learned about all of this while conducting routine background research on Sybil before she arrived in Maine. He packed a small arsenal of weapons that included handguns, rifles, and knives. He hoped he wouldn't have to use any of them. He never kept count of the people he had killed in combat. But he knew it had been a lot. It was part of the job. But he had no blood lust. He wanted to keep his clients safe without engaging in a fire fight.

It was after one in the morning when he finally went to bed. The house smelled of fresh paint. He didn't notice that someone had been watching his house for the past five hours.

28

"You're not who I was expecting," Sybil said upon seeing Sam for the first time at the Portland airport.

"What were you expecting?" Sam said as he picked up Sybil's bags and placed them in the back of his black Cadillac Escalade.

"Someone who is more of a brute. You look like you should be teaching high school," Sybil joked.

"I know how to take care of myself and you," Sam said. "Relax and enjoy the ride. We'll be there in the late afternoon. I contacted the caretaker Bess Croft to get the house ready. What's she like?"

"Bess is a kindly old woman who has known my father for years. The whispers in the family are that she and dad might have been lovers back in the day. But, of course, we would never say something like that out loud."

"It's never a good idea to be spreading rumors," Sam said.

"I'll keep that in mind," Sybil said.

"Were you afraid when the robbers broke into your house?"

"Fuck, yes," Sybil said.

"Do you really think they were robbers? Or were they after you? And was the break-in somehow related to the incident in South Dakota?"

"Those are three separate questions."

"Do you have any answers?"

"Not at the moment," Sybil said.

"What's your relationship like with your brother?"

"How do you get along with your siblings?" Sybil shot back.

"I'm an only child," Sam revealed.

"Lucky you," Sybil said. "Let's just say that Paul isn't as driven as me. Dad assigned him a division of the company that was doing very well and where he couldn't do much harm."

"How do you feel about being whisked away like this to a remote corner of Maine?"

"I usually like to stand my ground," Sybil said. "But dad insisted. He didn't like the press I was getting. More to the point, he didn't like the fact that his daughter was socially active. It didn't sit well with the political donor class with which he associates. That said, I also understand that something is going on. I don't want any harm to come to me either. It's called self-preservation."

"Always a good trait to possess," Sam said. "So, you and your dad don't see eye-to-eye politically?"

"That would be an understatement," Sybil said.

During the long drive north, Sam took a good look at Sybil while she sat in the passenger seat. She was of moderate height and had blond hair with a red tint to it. Her face was thin and symmetrical, as if shaped by a skilled sculptor. She had brooding brown eyes and long fingers, like those of a pianist. Sam wasn't sure if she was confident or arrogant. Probably a little of both, he thought. Over the years he came to learn that the privileged people only pretend to treat you as their equal. The reality was that they were loathe to allow you to enter into their tribe.

"Do you have weapons stored in the back?" Sybil said.

"This is my job. I need the tools of my trade," Sam said. "You wouldn't expect a plumber to come to your house without his wrenches."

"If you had to kill someone to keep me alive, would you?"

"Yes. But let's hope it doesn't come to that," Sam said.

"I'll sleep better at night knowing that you would kill for me."

"That's not something to joke about," Sam said.

"Sorry, Mr. Bodyguard," Sybil said sarcastically.

Sam turned off of the interstate and followed a series of increasingly narrow roads that eventually turned to dirt tracks. He came to a gate, which he had been told that the caretaker Bess had left unlocked. He had to exit the car to open and then close the metal gate. The Atwater house was located another mile ahead, through the dense pine forest.

The house was a hulking combination of wood and stone that was, nonetheless, tastefully done, Sam thought as he parked the Escalade. Bess walked out of the house and greeted Sybil and Sam.

"I'm Sam Rockland. Pleased to meet you."

"I'll show you to your room. Sybil knows where she'll sleep. She'll show you around while I fix us dinner," Bess said.

After dinner, Bess, Sybil, and Sam sat together in front of an impressive stone fireplace.

"I can't coax you into having a drink?" Sybil said.

"I'm on duty," Sam said.

"When are you off duty?"

"When my service is no longer required and I send your father a bill."

"Will it be a substantial one?"

"I don't come cheap," Sam said. He then stopped talking and sat upright. "Quiet, please."

"What is it?" Bess said.

"I hear cracking branches outside," Sam said. "Sybil, go upstairs please."

"Don't be ridiculous, it's probably a deer or a bear," Sybil said.

"I said go."

"OK. OK," Sybil muttered.

Sam grabbed a flashlight and a gun and opened the sliding door onto the back deck. The beam of light sliced through the darkness but did not reveal anything. Sam returned inside, making sure that all of the doors and windows were locked. He then went upstairs and knocked on Sybil's bedroom door.

"Did you see anything?"

"No. But I suggest that everyone turn in for the night."

"So, the party's over? Is that what you're saying?" Sybil said.

"Goodnight," Sam said, stifling a bemused smile.

***

He only went by the name of Cody. It wasn't his real name. He invented it to sound like 'coyote,' an animal that possessed cunning and survival skills in both urban and rural habitats that he admired.

He was heading to Millinocket, where he had reserved space in an RV park outside of town. He liked the fact that he could travel from place to place for his assignments pulling his small camper trailer behind his Ford truck. It gave him the freedom and anonymity he needed to do his job. He had driven cross country from South Dakota to northern Maine. He had done his job well near the Sioux reservation. His employer had been pleased. Although Cody felt a twinge of remorse having to kill a militia member whose ideology he sympathized with. But he didn't get to choose his targets. They were chosen for him. He didn't ask questions. He just cared that the money he had earned was deposited into his account in the Cayman Islands.

He settled into the space that the RV campground manager had assigned him. He would wait until nightfall to survey the location where his next target resided.

29

"Are we going to just sit in here all day?" Sybil said. "Is that the plan?"

"The plan is to keep you safe," Sam said. "Don't you have a business to run? You can do that from here. You have a phone and an internet connection."

"But I'm not used to being cooped up all day. Besides, no one knows I'm here. Can't we at least get outside for a while?" Sybil pleaded.

"Let me think about it," Sam said.

"Thank you for your consideration," Sybil snapped back.

***

Normally, Cody liked to find his target, eliminate it, and move on. But for this assignment, he was specifically told by his employer to instill fear into the intended target before killing it. Sadism was not something that typically appealed to Cody, but a job was a job and he was prepared to do what he had been asked.

Before arriving in Millinocket, he had gathered background information about Sheriff Buck Gastineau, who would be the first law enforcement officer to be involved once Cody set in motion his assignment. He needed Gastineau to keep out of his way. Cody knew just how to keep Gastineau in check. But that was for another day.

***

After two days in seclusion at the Atwater compound, Sam relented and suggested that he and Sybil go for a walk on one of the many trails that meandered through the family's vast acreage. It was late afternoon in the middle of August. Bess told them that dinner would be ready when they returned from their stroll.

"Some of the leaves are already beginning to turn," Sybil noted. "Autumn has always been my favorite season. It's as if nature were putting on a fashion show."

"That's very poetic," Sam noted.

"What moves you?"

"Competence and dedication," Sam said.

"That's a pretty dry set of criteria," Sybil said.

"I guess I'm a pretty dry guy."

"What do you do in your room all night? I see a light on well after midnight," Sybil said.

"You're spying on me now?"

"Just answer the question."

"I read books, sometimes in English, sometimes in another language. I'm partial to Spanish," Sam said.

"I visited Spain on a holiday during my university studies in London. I loved it. But I never had a knack for languages. Business strategy was more my thing," Sybil said.

"But you wrote your senior thesis on Native Americans. So, you're not all about numbers and deal making," Sam said. "You have a conscience."

"Thanks for noticing," Sybil laughed.

Sam checked his watch. "We should be getting back. We wouldn't want to keep Bess waiting."

Sam and Sybil looped back through the forest and returned to the house. They called out for Bess, but there was no answer as they entered the kitchen. There was no food being cooked.

"Stay here," Sam ordered.

Sam conducted a search of the entire house, but Bess was not there.

"Go down to the wine cellar, secure the door, and stay there until I return," Sam said.

"Where are you going?" Sybil said.

"I'm going to look around outside to see if I can find any signs of Bess. In the meantime, you can try calling her cell phone."

Sam nervously searched the perimeter of the house with his gun drawn. He found nothing. He was convinced, however, that someone had abducted Bess. She would not have wandered off on her own. He debated whether on not to call the local sheriff. He decided that he needed to. Before doing so, he escorted Sybil out of the wine cellar.

"Were you able to reach her?" Sam asked.

"No. What's going on?"

"Somebody is playing a game with us," Sam said.

***

"This is Sheriff Gastineau. Who is this?"

"Never mind who I am. Listen carefully to what I'm about to say. I have your daughter Shelley. I will not harm her. But you have to drag your feet on searching for a missing person whom you will soon learn about," Cody said.

"What the fuck are you talking about?"

"Just do what I say and Shelley will be fine."

"If I find out who you are, I'll fucking skin you alive," Buck said.

"You'll never get that chance."

***

"I know Bess. She's been around town for years now. She keeps good care of this place, Ms. Atwater," Buck said to Sybil after he arrived on the Atwater property. "Her cell phone must have run out of juice. I'm sure she's around here somewhere. I can't deploy a search team when she's just been gone a few hours. I don't have the resources."

"I understand your position," Sam interjected. "But I believe someone kidnapped and possibly killed Bess."

"And you are?"

"I'm Sam Rockland. I've been hired to protect Sybil against recent threats that she's received. I think Bess was taken to scare Sybil, to make her feel more anxious and frightened."

"Well, they succeeded," Sybil said.

"Are there any signs of forced entry to the house?" Buck said.

"No," Sam conceded.

"Let's wait until morning, then, before we all go nuts with conspiracy theories. If Bess doesn't turn up then, let me know. In the meantime, I can tell my patrol officers to keep an eye out for her," Buck said.

***

"Marty! Marty, get back here!" yelled Jeb Duncan at his dog who had run off from the trail on which they were walking.

Jeb scrambled to follow Marty into a dense thicket of weeds that, he feared, probably featured poison ivy as well as ticks.

"Damn it, Marty! Bad dog!" Jeb yelled again. Marty finally stopped and looked back at his master.

"Jesus Christ," Jeb muttered as he looked at what lay on the ground. It was a woman with her throat cut from ear to ear. Jeb thought for a moment about what law enforcement branch to call to report what he had discovered. He owned a cabin on a nearby lake that had been broken into several times. But the local sheriff had not done anything to solve the burglary. He thought that the county sheriff was at best lazy and at worse corrupt. He decided to dial the number for the state police instead.

***

Sometimes when she was alone at her house in Porcupine Haven, Nadine would turn around, thinking that her grandmother Martha was speaking to her. But there was no one there. Nadine still grieved the loss of Martha every day. A friend told her that she'll never really get over the loss; she had to be comforted by the memory of her grandmother. That image will never fade, Nadine was told by her friends. Nadine could conjure up an image of Martha, but at least for now, that did little to assuage her loneliness. She was about to prepare dinner for herself when she received a call from Captain Davies.

"A dog walker found a woman with her throat cut in a remote section of forest outside of Millinocket," Davies said. "The man contacted the state police directly."

"So, the sheriff is not aware that someone in his county has been murdered?"

"That's right. Do you want to contact Buck Gastineau, or should I?" Davies said.

"I will. I will relish the opportunity to tell him again to stay out of my way," Nadine said.

30

"Do we know who the victim is?" Nadine asked the forensics team lead.

"Yes. She was carrying her wallet and phone in her pants. It appears that nothing was stolen. Her name is Bess Croft. Her address indicates that she lived on a property just a few miles from here."

"Cause of death looks obvious," Nadine said.

"Yes, her neck was brutally severed with a serrated blade. She's probably been dead just a few hours."

"OK. I'll have to alert the local sheriff as a courtesy. There is a killer somewhere in this county. Transport the body to the medical examiner while I go to the address indicated on her driver's license."

Nadine entered the address into her phone to get directions to the remote property. As she drove to the Atwater compound, she phoned Buck Gastineau.

"Detective McAfee, you just can't stay away from this part of Maine," Buck said.

"I would stay away if it weren't for the fact that dead bodies keep turning up in your county," Nadine said.

"What do you mean?"

"I just left the scene of a murder. A woman named Bess Croft nearly had her head sliced off. I'm heading to her residence now. You never received a report of a missing woman?"

"Yes. I know Bess. She's the caretaker at the Atwater estate. The Atwater daughter named Sybil reported her missing earlier this evening," Buck confessed.

"And did you begin a search?"

"No. There were no signs of foul play and the house had not been broken into. I cautioned Ms. Atwater that we should wait for at least twenty-four hours before initiating a full-blown search."

"Well, that was clearly unwise," Nadine said. "I'll touch bases with you later tonight. I'm just about at the Atwater house. Shit, it's dark out here. I'd never find this place without a GPS."

Nadine stopped her SUV at the gate, which was open. She saw lights in the distance. She pulled up to the large house. The first person to emerge was a man. She noticed that he had a holstered gun. She opened her car door and flashed her badge.

"I'm Detective McAfee of the Major Crimes Unit. I'm looking for Sybil Atwater."

"She's in the house. I'm Sam Rockland, security consultant. Is this about Bess Croft?"

"Yes."

"She's dead, isn't she?"

"Yes."

"Come in, please," Sam said.

"How did you know that Bess was dead? What's going on here?" Nadine said.

"Sybil has been receiving death threats from an unknown source," Sam explained. "Her father hired me to protect her at this remote location. But, clearly, we were followed. Bess was abducted in the late afternoon to incite fear in Sybil and for the assassin to announce his presence."

"Where was Bess found?" Sybil said.

"About five miles from here. A dog walker discovered her body," Nadine said.

"We asked the sheriff to look for her," Sybil said, choking back tears. "But he wouldn't do it."

"I know all about that. I have my own history with Sheriff Gastineau," Nadine said. "Do you think you have things under control here, Mr. Rockland, or should I send a state police officer?"

"Call me Sam. Yes, the house is secure."

"Let me get your phone number so we can stay in touch," Nadine said. "I'll be based at the Moosehead Lodge during the investigation."

After Nadine departed the Atwater property, she contacted Captain Davies to fill him in on the situation.

"I need assistance contacting all lodgings in the county to learn who has checked in within the last forty-eight hours. The killer has to be staying somewhere," Nadine said.

"I'll assign someone to that task. But be careful. You're likely dealing with a professional hitman," Davies said.

***

"I told you that I needed you to delay the search for the missing woman," Cody said. "Now there are state police swarming all over the place."

"I followed your instructions. The woman was found by a dog walker, who called the state police number, not the county sheriff's office," Buck said. "Why did you kill Bess Croft?"

"Because I could."

"Where's my daughter?"

"She's safe for now."

"I swear that I'll kill you with my bare hands," Buck screamed into the phone.

"Keep dreaming, old man."

"I know the lead detective who has been assigned to the case. She's dogged. She'll track you down," Buck warned.

"I already know who it is. And I know how to deal with her. I'll be in touch," Cody said before hanging up.

Buck thought for a moment about what to do next. He figured that the man's last words were a cryptic threat against Detective McAfee. If he warned McAfee, however, he might be signing his daughter's death warrant. But then again, she might already be dead. He decided to contact McAfee. A portion of his conscience was still intact.

"Where are you now?" Buck asked.

"I'm in my room at the Moosehead Lodge," Nadine said.

"Stay there. I'll be right over. I have some information that may help you with the case."

Nadine waited for Buck in the lodge's lobby.

"What's this all about?" Nadine said.

"I've been in contact with Bess Croft's killer," Buck said. "He's kidnapped my daughter Shelley and is holding her somewhere. He told me to stay out of his way or he would kill her. He telegraphed what he was going to do with Bess. He told me to drag my feet about looking for her. I did. But then Bess's body was found quickly, and you became involved."

"The killer's real target is Sybil Atwater," Nadine said. "We're looking for him now."

"He's also looking for you," Buck said.

An explosion then rocked the lodge's parking lot. Windows shattered. Buck and Nadine dropped to the floor. Nadine could see a car burning outside. Nadine yelled to the night clerk to get every guest out of the lodge through the back door.

Nadine and Buck sprinted outside with guns drawn. As soon as they entered the parking lot, shots rang out from the woods. They hid behind parks cars, which were being peppered with rounds from a high-powered rifle. Buck and Nadine both called for backup. But then the fire fight ended as abruptly as it had begun.

Buck went to check on the lodge's guests and call the fire department. Nadine cautiously headed toward the woods from where the shots had been fired. She found spent cartridges on the ground. But she spotted no one. Her phone then buzzed.

"No one at the lodge was hurt. Just a few windows and nerves were shattered," Buck said upon his return.

"I think I may have found out where the killer has been staying. Do you know where the Arrowhead RV Park is?" Nadine said.

"Yes.

"Only one person has checked in there in the past two days. The manager said it was a middle-aged man with a buzz cut and a tattoo of an eagle on his right forearm," Nadine said.

"Let's go," Buck said.

"We'll take my car," Nadine said.

Nadine and Buck arrived at the RV park and walked to the manager's mobile home.

"The guy drove off earlier this evening in his truck. But he left his camper behind. It's parked in space number eight, by the public showers," the manager said.

Nadine and Buck started to walk toward the camper. Buck was the first person to hear the screams of a woman coming from inside it.

"It's Shelley," Buck said, as he jogged toward the camper.

"Wait, Buck!" Nadine yelled.

But she could not stop Buck, who rushed toward the camper and pulled open its door. The explosion blew Nadine back ten feet in the air. She looked at her jeans, which had been shredded by shrapnel. Her ears rang. But she still had all of her limbs. She tried to get up, but she fell back onto the gravel. The blast had disintegrated the camper, whose remnants were now burning.

The RV manager and a few of the other guests at the park helped Nadine up and dragged her farther away from the fire. Nadine could feel blood dripping down her legs. A woman wrapped a blanket around her shoulders. She sat dazed on the ground as the sound of sirens drew closer.

31

The EMTs arrived on the scene of the explosion along with the fire department, which quickly worked to extinguish the flames licking what remained of the shredded camper.

"We need to get you to the hospital to remove the shrapnel from your legs," one of the EMTs told Nadine. "You were very lucky. Your wounds are superficial, but you'll need a few stitches in several places."

Nadine's head still pounded and her body was sore all over. She was going to get into an ambulance to be taken to the hospital when her phone buzzed. There was a text from Sam Rockland that read: "He's here."

"I have to go," Nadine said, stepping out of the ambulance and discarding the blanket from her shoulders.

"You need to go to the hospital," the EMT said forcefully.

"I'll live," Nadine said, as she hobbled to her SUV. Her jeans were shredded and stained with blood.

She texted Sam that she was on her way to the Atwater property. Her legs burned as she drove along the dark, empty dirt roads. She stopped in front of the gate and exited her car. She could hear gunfire in the distance. She crept through the forest until the Atwater house came into view. She could feel blood dripping down her wounded legs.

She saw muzzle flashes from where the assassin was shooting into the Atwater house with a barrage of bullets from a high-powered automatic rifle. She could also see that Sam was returning fire from an elevated position on the house's second floor. She texted Sam that she was going to try to outflank the shooter.

As she approached the shooter, she tripped over a tree root and fell hard to the ground, compounding the pain in her legs. The shooter heard the noise and aimed his fire at her. His bullets riddled the trees above her; she stayed flat on the ground. Then she saw the shooter moving toward the corner of the house, where he placed an object on the ground; he retreated quickly. An explosion rocked the property, sending wood and glass flying into the air and starting a fire. The shooter was trying to force Sam and Sybil out of the burning house where he could then kill them.

Nadine arose from the forest floor and maneuvered to the back of the shooter's position. She finally saw a stocky man in a T-shirt aiming his weapon at the house, waiting for his targets to emerge. She yelled at the man, who turned around and fired at her. Multiple rounds rocketed into the tree trunks. Nadine returned fire, hitting the man, who fell to the ground. Nadine cautiously approached him. He lay groaning on the ground, wounded in his shoulder and abdomen. Nadine grabbed the rifle from the man and walked toward the burning house.

"The shooter is down!" Nadine yelled.

Sam and Sybil emerged from the house, coughing but unharmed.

"You're wounded," Sam said to Nadine. "Let's move away from the house. Where's the shooter?"

"About ten yards to the right. He's bleeding out from a gut wound," Nadine said. "Call for backup."

Sybil assisted Nadine, who had difficulty walking toward an open patch of lawn. Nadine then collapsed from a combination of exhaustion and pain. After checking on the condition of the shooter, Sam returned and covered Nadine's torso with his jacket,

"You're looking at the woman who saved our lives," Sam said to Sybil.

***

"You're looking better," Sam said while visiting Nadine in her hospital room.

"I still look and feel like shit," Nadine said. For the first time she noticed how handsome Sam Rockland was. The antibiotics and pain killers hadn't affected her eyesight. Although she felt embarrassed to be talking to him with unwashed hair and while wearing an unattractive hospital gown.

"How long will you be here?" Sam said.

"Just another day. But I'm pissed that I wasn't able to interrogate the shooter after he had come out of surgery. Captain Davies told me the whole story," Nadine said.

"Have you been brought up to speed about the conspiracy against Sybil?"

"Yes. The assassin who went by the moniker Cody was really Colt Brewer, an ex-CIA operative who was hired by Sybil's brother Paul to kill Sybil. With Sybil out of the picture, Paul could not only take over the family business but also be in line for a multi-million-dollar inheritance. Paul's political beliefs drew him into the sketchy world of white supremacists and militias. His hatred for Sybil was fueled as much by political ideology as it was by sibling rivalry," Sam said.

"How is Sybil?" Nadine said.

"Shocked, of course. But she's handling the revelations with her characteristic haughtiness. It's her father who is having a hard time reconciling what happened. He fears the negative publicity of a prolonged trial of his son for conspiracy to commit murder. He's encouraging Paul to plead guilty and spare the family any more embarrassment," Sam said.

"It's all about image, I guess," Nadine said, adding: "How do you feel about Sybil after spending so much time with her?"

"Attractive, yet arrogant. Not my type," Sam said.

"You have a type?" Nadine said.

"Someone whom I can count on," Sam said.

***

A week after being released from the hospital, Nadine looked at herself in the mirror. Her legs still contained stitches, but the bruising and pain had subsided. The doctor said that the scarring would be minimal. She phoned Captain Davies.

"I think I'd like to take some of the vacation that you owe me," Nadine said.

"I have no objection to that," Davies said. "You should go on a Caribbean cruise, or something like that."

"Actually, I'm going to drive down to Portland. I hear its beautiful there this time of year," Nadine said, smiling to herself as she looked at the series of texts she had received from Sam Rockland.

Made in the USA
Coppell, TX
12 December 2024

42407833R00128